Painted Death
A Kira Logan Mystery

Painted Death

A Kira Logan Mystery

J. C. Andrew

PAINTED DEATH
A KIRA LOGAN MYSTERY

This is a work of fiction. All of the characters, names, incidents, organizations, and dialogue in this novel are either the products of the author's imagination or are used fictitiously.

iUniverse books may be ordered through booksellers or by contacting:

iUniverse
1663 Liberty Drive
Bloomington, IN 47403
www.iuniverse.com
1-800-Authors (1-800-288-4677)

Because of the dynamic nature of the Internet, any web addresses or links contained in this book may have changed since publication and may no longer be valid. The views expressed in this work are solely those of the author and do not necessarily reflect the views of the publisher, and the publisher hereby disclaims any responsibility for them.

ISBN: 978-1-4917-4531-1 (sc)
ISBN: 978-1-4917-4533-5 (hc)
ISBN: 978-1-4917-4532-8 (e)

Library of Congress Control Number: 2014915974

Print information available on the last page.

iUniverse rev. date: 09/08/2016

ACKNOWLEDGEMENTS

My thanks go to:

Dot Bardarson, who took a chance and introduced me to the magic of Alaska and its people.

The members of the Seward Mural Society, who so graciously welcomed me.

Kris Neri for her inspirational critique.

The Village Writers group, with their enlightening and humbling comments and support.

And especially to Willma Gore, who helped and encouraged me to turn from artist to author.

CHAPTER ONE

The weather rapidly deteriorated, making the inside passage rougher than forecast. Gale force winds and unpredictable waves caused the boat, *Halibut Hunter*, to veer erratically. At sixty-one feet and seaworthy enough, it was still a bitch to handle in choppy water or following seas. Constant attention to the wheel left little time for rest or food. Concentration was difficult enough during the day. Tonight was hell, with limited vision and only softly-lighted instruments for guidance.

Jason Tideman desperately wanted to close his eyes for a few minutes rest. He knew he dared not give in to that wish, as even a few moments of inattention could be the last ones of his life. Anchoring in some cove for the night for a short break was another possibility. After considering what he knew of his present employers, that idea seemed even more dangerous than continuing in his current sleep-deprived state. He would have to depend on the wind and intermittent rain to keep slapping him awake.

Randy, his new crewman, might be able to take a watch, but Jason knew almost nothing about the kid and feared he was too inexperienced a navigator to be reliable in harsh weather, or if he knew enough to use the autopilot. He wasn't sure Randy, with his apathetic attitude, would be reliable, even on a calm, sunny day.

More than a month before, Randy had approached Jason in his homeport of Raven Creek, Alaska. Jason had been working on his boat to prepare for the fishing season and the soon-to- arrive tourists and fishermen from the lower forty-eight, who dreamed of catching the big one. Being a charter boat captain paid the bills in the summer. Winter was another matter. Money was damned scarce by early spring. So in the good months, all charter captains worked their asses off.

Randy was a tall, thin, long-haired, rather unkempt young man. He said an associate, who knew Jason was interested in "extra" cash, had recommended he contact him. In the privacy of the *Halibut*'s cabin, Randy proposed a trip to Seattle to pick up a special cargo. Jason, realizing who was behind Randy's "proposal," knew he really had no option but to go. Even so, he hesitated, saying, "It's a long way and that particular cargo could get me into lots of trouble if anyone found out."

Randy's casual, "whatever" acceptance of Jason's reluctant agreement to the trip, as well as his insistence upon acting as crew, dismayed Jason. But when the probable amount of the "extra" was mentioned, as well as the necessity for going, Jason couldn't turn him down, even though he was dead against the cargo he would bring in. It was possible that this might be the first of many trips. If successful and the "source" was satisfied, his finances would receive a welcome boost. Unfortunately, his need for the extra money exceeded his distaste for the cargo. He could see no option but to go along.

Jason was aware of the danger in the plan. Hell, anyone would be unless they had been shipwrecked on an atoll for fifty years. The law-abiding public, much less the police, and especially the DEA, did not sanction smuggling. Drugs were an increasing problem in Alaska. The newspapers and TV were always going on about the dangers of marijuana, heroin, or meth.

The thought of the drug dealers he would be working for made him nervous. Not a reliable or safe group of people; in fact, deadly if he screwed up. But that money . . . one had to think of the future. Those thousands would sure be useful.

After picking up the "cargo" in Seattle, Jason planned to travel north to Fort Madding with three stopovers for fueling. In Raven Creek he would refuel again and perhaps have time with his family before the remainder of the trip.

Randy spoke to his handler about the layover, who argued strongly against the plan. "The boss won't be happy until the hand-over of the goods," Randy reported.

Reminding himself that he was still the captain, Jason thought it to his advantage to assert his bargaining position. He said, with somewhat spurious confidence, "Your boss should stick to his part of the business. I know the ways of the water and the abilities of the *Halibut Hunter*. I'll handle my part. We'll put into Raven Creek. Besides, if I'm away too long, there might be questions raised. I intend to do some fishing. A fish or two will be useful to provide an excuse for this long run." Randy made it obvious he didn't like this independent streak. However, to Jason's relief, he didn't argue, just gave him a long look.

This trip would allow him to pay all his bills with plenty left over.

* * *

Jason brought the *Halibut Hunter* south from Raven Creek, Alaska, to a small dock north of Seattle. After picking up their special cargo and waiting until the small hours of the morning, when the dock was quiet and the surrounding waters empty of traffic, they untied the boat and quietly disappeared into the darkness.

As the *Halibut Hunter* moved north, and approached Raven Creek and Otter Bay, the rough weather finally moderated. Jason noticed Randy speaking in a low voice on the satellite phone. The worried look on his face and his rigid stance made him appear to be arguing. Then he said, "All right, I suppose that would work." A few minutes later he wandered into the pilothouse and informed Jason that there would be a boat waiting at Simmon Bay by Ragan Island. They were to come in after dark, around 2330 hours, so the goods could be transferred and paid for. By then other boats with their watchful crews should already be in the harbor, seventeen nautical miles away.

"That's strange," Jason said, his voice worried. "How come the pickup is happening down here? The plan was to meet near Fort Madding in six more days. What's going on?"

Randy shrugged off the questions. "I'm just telling you what the boss said. I can't read his mind. I do what he orders, and you'd better do the same."

Jason looked at his departing back with disgust.

Shortly after 2300 hours they rounded Barnstable Island, turning north into Otter Bay. Soon they sighted Ragan Island and the entrance to Simmon Bay. The water, still running high from the storm, calmed as the boat entered the bay. To starboard the running lights of another vessel could be seen near the island. The more protected water provided a good place for a transfer, if this was what was planned. But it hadn't been the original plan, and Jason didn't like the abrupt change. The men he was dealing with weren't trustworthy on the best of days. Meeting late at night, in a dark, lonely location, was asking for trouble.

The moon's light momentarily filtered through a rift in the clouds. Jason could see the other vessel's fenders were out. He instructed Randy to deploy theirs—at least the kid could do that—and tie up to the other boat. Except for their running lights and a slight glow from the pilothouse, it was dark on the other deck. Jason could barely discern three figures in dark jackets waiting motionless at the rail.

One of the men called Jason's name. When he answered and identified himself, the man called them to "come aboard." Jason wasn't about to leave the *Halibut Hunter* while lying concealed in a secluded cove, in darkness, with the load on board that he was carrying. *He can damn well come to me!*

The man finally boarded the *Halibut Hunter* with reluctance and loud swearing. His features were difficult to make out in the darkness but, with surprise, Jason recognized him. He was somewhere in his forties, a big man in height and weight, with a broad face and a developing paunch under his unbuttoned jacket. His angry expression made clear that this was not a social occasion and he didn't like Jason's attitude. He wanted the transaction completed, and fast.

"Where the hell you been? You taken long enough to get here," the big man demanded.

"The weather was rough coming up," Jason replied. "Then the fishing took extra time. What did you expect?" *God, didn't this thug realize that, good boat or not, I had to deal with the rotten weather and distance?*

With a grunt the big man glanced at the cargo, then called one of his men to come on board and help Randy make the transfer while he completed financial arrangements in the cabin.

Dropping the bag containing the money on the counter, he asked, "Two hundred kilos of heroin and eighteen bales of marijuana. Right?" His teeth showed in a momentary, predatory grin.

"Just right," Jason replied, his eyes moving to the bag.

"Any trouble at the other end?"

"No. The dock was quiet and the goods were waiting."

"You tell anyone where you were going this trip?"

"Are you kidding? I didn't mention it to anyone.

"Good. We don't want people to know where you went. People might talk. We wouldn't want that, would we?" His grim look boded a short future for anyone who might say too much.

"You don't have to worry," Jason quickly assured him. "I have no desire to spend the rest of my life in a cell, inadequately supported by angry taxpayers."

"No," the boss said. "We will have to be real sure that don't happen to you, won't we? None of my movers has ever gone to prison. I don't intend you to be the first."

"Glad to hear that," Jason mumbled.

"Now to business. Since you have all the merchandize, our agreed price still stands. The cash's here. You can count it if you want, but I don't short my people, and they had better not short me."

Feeling a need to assert his independence, Jason said, "Since this is my first time on this run, I think I'll check to be sure the count is right."

The big man raised an eyebrow, but said nothing. Uneasily Jason opened the bag and took a careful count of the bills. "Looks OK to me," he said. *Why did I do that? A misguided moment of quivering macho perhaps? God knows what I would have done if the right amount of money had not been there.*

"That's all right then," the big man said. Jason didn't like his smile.

Back on the now deserted deck, Jason welcomed the fresh air. The cabin had been stuffy with danger, threat, and, Jason had to confess, fear. *My God! Why did I ever get involved with this group? Is the money worth it?*

The cargo transferred, it was past time for Randy to come back on the *Halibut*. Jason heard him talking with one of the men. Then a quick laugh. *Can't he do anything right? What is taking him so long?* Jason looked back at the moneyman. In the dark he could make out the sneering grin on his face. To his horror he saw something else. Gripped in the man's large hand was . . . oh God . . . a gun. It looked enormous . . . and it was pointed at him!

"What's going on?" Jason cried. But he already knew the answer. *What a fool I've been, not being willing to work by their rules as to a nonstop trip, asserting my imaginary freedom of choice. They didn't rely on me after all. They could have trusted my judgment. They should have. Damn! Damn! Da . . .!*

The pain was incredible. He had been injured before; no one working on ships can avoid it, but this was beyond anything he'd ever experienced. Jason collapsed onto the deck, his face smashing on the wood, the smell of fish scales and salt water in his nose, and knew this was as far as he was going. He heard, as from a distance, the big man barking out orders.

"Randy. Get back on this tub. Take it out to deep water and sink it."

"Sink it? How do I do that?" Randy whined.

"Oh my God. Don't you know anything! Go down and cut out sections of the rubber hose leading from the sea-cocks. I have a saw you can use. It will take an hour or so for the boat to go under once the water starts coming in. We'll be right behind you and pick you up before it sinks. Then we can all get out of here."

"You'd better be near. The water here is too fuckin' cold to swim in!"

The last thing Jason heard was the big man saying thoughtfully, "It is, isn't it? Forty degrees or less. A body wouldn't last long in that." His voice sharpened. "Just get going and do what you're told." With that he reached into the *Halibut's* cabin, grabbed the bag of money, and climbed back onto the other boat.

CHAPTER TWO

Friday

The email to Kira Logan arrived in July. "His body's been found . . . with a bullet mark on one of the ribs. Rumors of murder and smuggling are flying around town. Local people don't want the dead man's boat, *Halibut Hunter*, included in your design. We'll discuss our options when you arrive."

Alarmed, Kira emailed back quickly to ask her old friend for more details, but Jackie Denton was unwilling to clarify the situation further.

A freelance artist, Kira lived in a secluded town north of Phoenix, Arizona. The endless hours invested in preparing all the art pieces for an early spring show of her work in a Tucson gallery had left her exhausted. The call from Jackie, an art school friend and member of the Raven Creek, Alaska Mural Society, came at the perfect time. Jackie had contacted her to learn if she was interested in designing a mural for them. Titled "Lost Mariners of Raven Creek," it was to be a tribute to the captains and crews from the port, that had been lost at sea. A moment's thought was all it took for Kira to reply with an enthusiastic and grateful, "Yes."

Jackie had immediately inundated Kira with photos and web references of sunken ships, maps of the waters where the ships had gone down, and individual histories of the boats and their captains. *Halibut Hunter,* the most recently lost boat, was included in that list, even though, at that time, there was still no definite knowledge of its fate.

Kira spent many hours researching the various craft, then worked to arrange her design to show each boat's shape, and, when possible, location, and the way it was destroyed. Since the mural would be large enough to cover the outside wall of a building, there was ample space to indicate a storm for ships that sank from the weather, as well as areas of fog for boats that had disappeared mysteriously. She placed the still-missing *Halibut Hunter* in the latter area, thinking that when more was known, she could either move it to the appropriate place or remove it, if the local people were too upset about its inclusion. When the design was completed, Kira sent Jackie a copy for approval by the Mural Society.

Jackie said the mural would be produced using local volunteer painters—Kira hoped that wasn't as chancy as it sounded—and take place during the Raven Creek Music Festival in September. The mural would be painted at that time to make it a part of the community celebrations, gain supporters for the project, and make it easy to schedule volunteers. Jackie laughingly described the music festival, with obvious affection, as a rowdy gathering of folk music performers, dancers, acrobats, improbable culinary concoctions, and crafts, only to be seen in small Alaskan towns and villages.

Now it was September, and Kira had just landed in Anchorage, Alaska, joyfully anticipating seeing her friend for the first time in years. She would stay with Jackie and her husband, Warren, while she oversaw the work necessary to turn her mural idea into a reality. The problems waiting in Raven Creek concerned Kira. The uncertainty Jackie referred to was casting a shadow over what Kira expected to be a working, but still relaxing, getaway to a small town in a beautiful setting.

When they met in the Anchorage airport, Jackie and Kira hugged and immediately launched their catching-up talk. At five-feet-four, Jackie was five inches shorter than Kira. In art school, people had often commented on the physical differences between the two close friends. Jackie's short, dark, wavy hair and pixie quickness were a contrast to Kira's slim, five-foot-nine height, red-blond hair, and thoughtful manner.

Out in the fresh northern air, blown in over the ocean and cooled by the snow-clad mountains, Kira's spirits soared. She felt lighthearted and ready to begin her eagerly contemplated Alaskan adventure.

They drove south from the airport, along a highway that barely clung to the cliffs bordering Turn-Again Arm, an extension of water from Cook Inlet and Chickaloon Bay. The scenery awed Kira. The low tide exposed tantalizing abstract designs of sandbars capable of swallowing unwary wandering tourists foolish enough to venture out on them.

Jackie and Kira spent the first part of the drive filling in details of their lives since they'd last talked. Their friendship had begun over twenty years before in a California art school, where they'd shared a dormroom, struggled and laughed through all the outrageous class assignments, and finally celebrated success with their friends at graduation. Two years ago Jackie had remarried and now lived with her husband in Raven Creek, a small fishing and tourist town south of Anchorage.

During a lull in the conversation, Kira asked, "How are the mural preparations coming? Are the town's people pleased with my design?"

"It's all going very well," Jackie replied. "The metal panels we'll be painting were delivered this week and are safely locked in the terminal building where we'll work."

She added, "There is the one difficulty I warned you about that may affect your design."

This was the opening Kira was waiting for. "Did they find the missing boat, or has something else come up since we last talked?" *Jackie must know my question was not about metal panels.*

"The boat is still missing."

Pressed for more information, Jackie was evasive, stubbornly insisting that this was the time to "Relax, enjoy the drive, and become acquainted with the glories of 'my home turf.' "

Kira persisted. "I thought the design was set. The project hasn't been cancelled, has it?"

Jackie smiled and silently pointed to the scenery.

Kira took the hint and, looking out the car window, had to admit Jackie's turf was indeed glorious. Mountains loomed on both sides of the valley; their lower parts covered with fireweed, low and high bush Cranberries, and Devil's Club, a large leafed plant armed with vicious spines. It was a short rise in elevation to the tree line, where gray and forbidding rocks protruded, their barren surfaces brightened occasionally by small hidden pockets of snow that had escaped the sun. Rocky edges of peaks were jagged against the pale blue sky, the sharp outlines of the summits scarcely modified by time or weather.

Kira scanned the bushes looking for the moose, bear, or Dall sheep she had read about. After miles of searching the surrounding hills she had to admit that, when it came to mammals, her luck was out. The only animals in abundance were birds. Jackie told her the Tundra swans, resting on a lake, would soon be migrating. Ravens were ever-present in the air, or checking the road for a tasty gift from a passing car. As they neared Raven Creek, Kira glimpsed bald eagles drifting overhead, eyes alert for a meal. She was almost ready to sing "The Star-Spangled Banner" until their image was slightly tarnished in her mind by Jackie informing her that the magnificent birds were scavengers of carrion as well as hunters of fish.

CHAPTER THREE

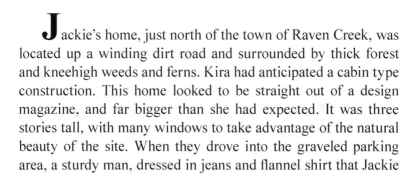

Jackie's home, just north of the town of Raven Creek, was located up a winding dirt road and surrounded by thick forest and kneehigh weeds and ferns. Kira had anticipated a cabin type construction. This home looked to be straight out of a design magazine, and far bigger than she had expected. It was three stories tall, with many windows to take advantage of the natural beauty of the site. When they drove into the graveled parking area, a sturdy man, dressed in jeans and flannel shirt that Jackie described as the uniform of the area, came out of the house.

"Kira, I'd like you to meet Warren, my 'Treasure of the North' that I told you about." Jackie grinned like a lucky prospector who'd suddenly found gold. Warren looked to be in his early forties, with wavy hair, and smile lines embedded in his cheeks.

He stepped forward to shake hands, his grip firm, expression welcoming. "My wife has been looking forward to your arrival and working with you on her 'little project.' " He smiled, glancing at Jackie.

"Little?" Jackie retorted. "Little! This mural Kira designed will be sixteen feet tall by fifty-six feet wide, and make an impressive addition to those already mounted on other buildings here in Raven Creek." She looked up at him with mock disgust. "Little indeed!"

Warren smiled and affectionately put his arm around her. "My rocket-propelled lady has been eagerly counting the days until your arrival, planning typical Alaskan activities to reward you for all the work she expects you to do this coming week. In spite of the labor to come, I think you'll enjoy what's ahead." Warren looked down at Jackie and hugged her. "She's worked for months to ensure that this project will be as trouble-free as possible—she doesn't want you to regret your decision to engage in the coming chaos. But why stand out here? You two go inside and get settled. I'll put the car away and bring in your luggage."

The home's hand-carved wooden front door depicted jumping salmon in low relief. "Good heavens. I wasn't expecting a mansion!" Kira exclaimed as she followed Jackie toward the entrance. "I thought everyone up here lived in cozy log cabins covered with moss and snow."

"The early settlers did, and many still do. But a whiff of civilization and progress has come in," Jackie said, and laughed, as they walked inside. "Let me give you a quick tour, then we can sit down and continue catching up on all the news."

The first space they entered was a work and storage area. Jackie explained that life up north demanded adjustments in housing design. "In winter," she said, "mud and snow are such huge problems that many homes are built with maintenance areas on the ground floor."

The kitchen, dining, and great room, as well as a bath, and guest room for Kira's use, were on the second floor. A well-used fireplace filled one corner of the large room. Native crafts, as well as some of Jackie's artwork, decorated the wood paneled walls or stood on various display pedestals. Colored rugs were scattered about. "They brighten the room on gray days, as well as provide warmth for feet in winter months," Jackie said.

As she looked around the spacious living area, Kira said, "I'd no idea homes up here could be so comfortable. The guest room is very inviting, and I can't wait to get a closer look at all the art you've been doing since I last saw you."

"I paint quite a bit and still have time for other activities," Jackie said. "This may be a small isolated community, but we don't spend the winters locked in our homes. We have a group that puts on plays, and another that gives musical performances. Then there are all the outside sports, like skiing, snowshoeing, and dog-sledding. In spite of the long hours of darkness, snow, and cold, our lives are never dull."

After a quick trip to the third floor to see Warren and Jackie's office and their bedroom, the two women returned to the kitchen. "Now that you've had the tour, we'll make some tea, grab a plate of veggies, and sit on the deck to enjoy the pleasant weather," Jackie said. Outside, they settled into comfortable armchairs to share a spectacular view of Otter Bay and the mountains beyond.

Kira sighed with pleasure and turned to Jackie. "You two have a beautiful place here, with those imposing mountains, the distant water, the sense of endless space—it's incredible. And I'm happy to finally meet Warren. Your descriptions of him made him sound like a combination of a knight of old and the latest movie sensation. Now, I see you weren't exaggerating."

Jackie's face had a gentle, contented expression. "I feel lucky to have found him," she said. "As I wrote you, I was ready to swear off all men after my first marriage ended so badly."

"You were never clear about what happened. You said you'd had enough, and 'what's his name' could take a hike. He must have hiked pretty far. It's been three years, hasn't it, since you wrote about him?"

"Four since he blessedly departed. You may not know it, but drugs are a big problem in this state. When I found he was selling the stuff to the local kids, I acted fast. I just wanted him out of my life, so I promised to say nothing if he would agree to a divorce and quickly leave town." She spread her hands in seeming wonder at her previous foolishness. "I must have been nuts to marry him in the first place. I wish now I had reported him. His was an evil trade."

As they talked, two jays hopped from branch to branch in the mountain laurel tree near the deck, landed on the deck railing, and bounced over to the seeds and peanuts placed there for them. "Well, it's all behind you now," Kira said. "I like Warren, and he certainly seems to appreciate you. His office looks very businesslike, especially with his computers spread around on those beautiful wood cabinets," she said. "What work does he do there, or does he just sit and admire the view?"

"Both I imagine." Jackie laughed. Then more seriously she said, "But it's mostly work. He sets up websites for businesses all over Alaska, as well as for some in the lower forty-eight. I don't claim to understand all the details, but he keeps involved and busy. The best part is the flexibility it gives him. When I need help, or a special occasion arises, he can be available.

Warren emerged from the guest room where he had taken Kira's luggage. After a few minutes in the kitchen to open a bottle of wine and load a tray with glasses and plates of crackers, cheese, and fruit, he came out to the porch and passed the tray around. With an impish grin he said, "I overheard the last of what you were saying. The truth is, Jackie directs my life now. She's more demanding than any boss could ever be."

"Not likely." Jackie laughed up at him. "Warren is his own man when it comes to his work."

Kira said, "I'm excited to begin mine. What do I need to know to be useful while I'm here."

"There will be plenty for you to do," Jackie said. "If previous years are any indication, the schedule will have to be adjusted to work around minor mechanical disasters, painting mistakes, and no-show volunteers."

Warren asked Jackie, "Have you told her yet?" Then he looked at Kira. "She doesn't want to admit, even to herself, that there may be people who are dissatisfied with the image of the *Halibut Hunter* being in your mural design. It's an issue that could become serious. I think it's time you're told about the dispute." He moved to the edge of the deck, brushed aside the birdseed and peanuts on the wide railing, then settled into a chair and put his feet up on the cleaned space. Jackie now lay stretched out on two chairs, taking advantage of the late afternoon sun that would too soon disappear.

Kira said, "Tell me about the problem. Jackie wouldn't say anything on the drive here."

"She probably wanted to avoid talking about it until you were here and settled in."

Jackie opened her eyes, shading them from the sun. "I've warned her." She glanced at her husband as though unsure which of them should begin. Then, sitting up, she faced Kira and said, "The mural committee has been talking with local people about this year's painting, trying to sign up more volunteers to paint." She sighed. "All the publicity we generated helps. The subject matter is well known and long overdue.

"Since Raven Creek surrounds the north end of Otter Bay, life here is naturally focused on the water and the boats that use it. Other than tourism, our economy is largely dependent on shipping and fishing. Because of this, we thought finding people to help paint a mural about the history of the bay would be easy." She frowned as she leaned forward to choose another cracker.

"That makes sense to me," Kira said. "The subject should have wide appeal. What went wrong?" All this roundabout talk was making her fear that Jackie had understated the problem in order to keep her arrival upbeat.

"Some people are reluctant to help because of the subject," Warren said.

"Ships and captains from Raven Creek who have lost their boats and their lives—what could be wrong with that subject?" Kira asked. "I think the idea of honoring them is a good one."

Warren refilled her wine glass. She felt the need for it. So far this conversation was going nowhere.

Jackie shrugged. "Oh, it is . . . was," she replied. "But something has come up that a few critics don't like very much. It involves the local boat, *Halibut Hunter*. Some people think it should not be included in the painting."

That's weird. It was one of the boats lost just this year. "It's in my design that the mural committee approved," Kira said. "Why would it not qualify for the mural, or has the boat been found?"

"No, it's still missing," Warren replied. "However, there is a rumor going around town concerning the *Halibut's* captain. Some think the captain, Jason Tiedemann, wasn't simply fishing. It seems strange to many that, so far as is known, he had no clients with him on his trip, just one crew member, and he was away too long. No captain takes his boat out without carrying paying customers. Thus, the question arises, what else might he have been doing?" He paused dramatically. "Some are suggesting he was smuggling drugs. His friends say that is nonsense."

This surprised Kira. "Jumping to conclusions with very little information, aren't they?" It seemed to her that mob thinking might be beginning. To clarify the situation for her own understanding she asked, "And you say he wasn't alone?"

"We don't think so. Rumor places someone named Randy with him. It seems the two barely knew each other and had never worked together. Lots of the people wonder why Jason would choose him for such an extended trip. Of course, it may have been intended to be no more than a one-day trip. The boat could have gone down anywhere, anytime."

"How long was it before someone reported their absence?"

"No one can definitely say when they disappeared." Jackie said, passing the snack tray to Kira. "He had a family. There's a wife, Selena, Vin, his son, and a daughter, Angela. It was nearly a week before his wife reported his absence. They've all said they knew nothing about what he was doing, or his destination. Apparently, Jason didn't tell them where he was going, or why, and they said he made no attempt to communicate with his family while he was away."

This seemed strange to Kira. Would someone plan a long voyage with deck help he barely knew, and keep secret his destination or schedule? She understood why this would have people wondering. But drugs? That was quite a reach with almost no evidence. "Well, if not to his family, did he say anything to his fishing buddies before he left? He must have talked about the trip with someone."

"No one has come forward that we've heard about," Jackie replied.

"The boat was last seen sometime in early April," Warren continued. He looked toward the bay, pausing, as though to organize his facts. "Then in July, a call came into the Anchorage Coast Guard informing them that something was caught on the rocks southwest of Raven Creek, attracting flocks of seagulls, fish, and several seals. The caller couldn't clearly discern the object, but thought it might be a stranded orca or a dead sea lion—some type of meat, to judge from the activities of the encircling marine life.

"The story I've heard is that the Anchorage office contacted the one in Raven Creek, asking that the object be identified, and mentioned their records showed a local boat, the *Halibut Hunter,* that couldn't be accounted for. Then Anchorage went on to suggest that, if it was the captain's body, the Raven Creek office might institute another search for his boat in nearby bays or inlets."

Jackie explained to Kira, "No one knew where the *Halibut Hunter* had gone down, or even if it had. Boat hijackers, as well as accidents and storms, have to be considered when a boat disappears. If talk in town is to be believed, the skipper may have had enough of his second wife's shenanigans and taken off to other ports. The word is that she spent too much money on clothes and entertainment and was constantly criticizing him, his children, and their lifestyle. With a repaint job on the boat name and hull identification number, he might disappear without a trace."

She leaned toward Kira, adding softly, "Then the Coast Guard found the captain's remains washed up on rocks outside the bay. They were almost unrecognizable." She paused, as though the vision in her mind was too horrible for her to accept. "We heard that the authorities couldn't make a positive identification until his dental records were checked. Between the storms and the animals in the bay, there wasn't much remaining of his face, or anything else, to help provide a name."

"How awful," Kira said, not wanting to imagine what the Coast Guard had found. "Does anyone know what happened to the other person? Has anyone seen him? He might not have been on the boat, after all. If he turned up, he could tell what occurred."

"Randy has not been accounted for," Warren said. "He disappeared, leaving no trace."

"So, I still don't understand. It's a sad story, but how does that affect the painting?" Kira couldn't comprehend their uncertainty. "What is there about his disappearance that could possibly concern us?"

"The problem is . . . the captain died from a gunshot wound," Warren answered. "They found the mark on his ribs."

After quietly considering his statement, Kira said, "Jackie did mention that to me in her email. It could indeed be a complication."

"Complication!" Jackie exclaimed, leaning forward. "It could be a disaster. We don't need this controversy or bad publicity." She was adamant. "The owners of the building where the mural will be installed aren't going to want a painting that offends the community. We don't want to be known as a town that not only encourages drug traffic, but glorifies the drug runners by honoring the boats they use for their dirty work."

"Now, I think you're overstating the case. It isn't that bad—at least not yet," Warren said soothingly.

"Have the police said what they think—suicide or a crime?" Kira asked, swirling the wine in her glass.

"The police haven't said anything decisive," Warren replied. He repositioned himself in his chair. "The Coast Guard won't commit to an answer either. Vin, his son, thinks he probably had a gun on board, but since neither the boat nor gun has been found, and may never be, it's impossible to make a final decision as to the source of the bullet."

"Even if they were to find the gun, with no bullet as evidence, it would be difficult to prove anything," Jackie interjected. "So either solution might be reasonable. His death could have been a suicide. But then again . . ."

Warren said, "All people do is talk, talk, talk. No one knows anything for sure." He stood up abruptly and crossed to stand in front of the railing.

"So you can imagine the rumors that are circulating," Jackie said, taking up the thread of the conversation, while she chose a clump of grapes from the plate. "People can't figure out why the *Halibut Hunter* was out that early in the season without a fishing client or anyone knowing where it was going. And since Randy's body has not been found, opinions are divided. Was he a victim, too, or the villain?"

Silence prevailed, as the three appeared to consider the question. Then Kira asked, "Did Randy seem the type to cause trouble? Would he have any reason to kill the captain?"

"I understand this was his first trip with Jason. No one knows much about him. He's a sort of mystery man," Jackie replied, idly rubbing her hand along the weathered arm of the chair.

"I've heard that Randy knew Jason's son, Vin," Warren said. "I have no direct knowledge on this point. I do know Vin didn't get on well with his father, but I can't imagine his being in league with an enemy and working against him." He left his position in front of the railing to return to his chair.

"Why didn't they get along?" Kira asked. "What was Jason like? Was he of the Captain Bly mentality?"

"I wouldn't say so," replied Warren slowly. "He was a hard worker and expected Vin to help on the *Halibut Hunter*. Unfortunately, Vin never showed much interest in boats or fishing. He went out with his father when he was a youngster—he hadn't much choice. As he got older he grew to resent his father's demands. From what I know of him, he was more interested in computers—programming and game development—than in outdoor activities."

"How did you learn all this?" Kira asked.

"We had a chance to talk about my work with websites when I was helping the computer club at the high school. He talked at great length about wanting to attend the local technical college. He didn't say it outright, but it's possible there may have been money problems that stood in the way of his going."

Kira was slightly confused. "I thought fishing boats were financially very successful, that chartering one was quite expensive. If that's true, why couldn't Vin's father help him with school costs?"

"You're right. Chartering used to be a good investment—if you owned your own boat and had plenty of customers," Warren said, nodding. "However, that's changed recently. The cost of fuel is rising rapidly, and fewer vacationers are coming. The wealthy seem to be immune to the financial realities of the rest of us, but there are not as many of them as there used to be. Those that do come can be more particular in their choice of boats." He spread his hands as if to express the hopelessness of the situation. "The boat Jason skippered was all right, but not a new one. It lacked some of the latest fish-finding gear. I wouldn't be surprised if he was having a difficult time getting clients."

They were again silent as they considered what Warren had said. Kira broke the quiet by asking, "What do you mean, 'skippered'? Wasn't the *Halibut Hunter* his boat?"

"No. He couldn't afford to own it outright," Jackie said. "The boat belonged to Owen Martin, a local investor and owner of the boatyard across the bay. He used the *Halibut Hunter* as a source of income and a tax advantage." Her expression lightened. "You'll be meeting him tomorrow."

Still trying to understand, Kira persisted. "Why would Jason's financial problems, or even his death, have anything to do with whether his boat is included in the mural? That seems irrelevant. Or is the controversy over the fact that he was shot and no one can determine how it happened?"

"Normally, neither would matter, Jackie continued, "but rumors have begun circulating that to save his financial life he might have taken to an illegal activity, such as smuggling. If that should be true, some of the town's people, or those in the Chamber of Commerce, may rebel at having his boat in the painting." She added, disdain in her voice, "They may only be interested in boats with pure reputations."

"Oh, come on!" Kira exclaimed. "How do they know what the other vessels portrayed in the mural were carrying when they went down . . . or what the crew or captains were like?" She felt slightly cynical. "After the research I did for this project, I doubt many of those vessels could pass the 'Raven Creek Purity Test' if they were closely examined."

"That's probably true," Warren agreed, flashing a grin. Then, serious again, he continued, "But those ships sank years ago. This one is recent, and people are still actively speculating. The case isn't closed, so people are liable to get upset if it turns out that Jason was acting illegally."

Kira's studies of the ships that had previously gone down had led her to believe that many strange and illegal items, ranging from protected animal skins and weapons, to gold and liquors, now lay at the bottom of the nearby waters. She was against the drug trade, but considered a small boatload of heroin or marijuana only an insignificant addition to what was already under the waves.

"This is supposed to be an historical record, not a moral monument." Jackie gestured with her wine glass, which fortunately was almost empty. "I don't know how Kira feels, but I believe we should go ahead with the painting as planned." She continued, "I think it's too early to make big decisions. There's nothing but rumor right now—not an adequate reason to change the design. And, just as important, no one is, as yet, threatening a withdrawal of funds from the project."

Kira said, "I worked hard on that plan and the mural society approved it. I think we should continue with the original idea. If we meet with overwhelming resistance we can always paint out the *Halibut Hunter* later. Who knows? It will probably turn out that the skipper was doing nothing wrong, and this controversy will fade away." She hoped she was right.

CHAPTER FOUR

Jackie, Warren, and Kira talked through dinner and late into the evening about what had happened in their lives during the years they had been apart. Jackie asked about Kira's two children, Kelly and Forest. "They are independent of me, living on their own. Forest is in Denver, where he works as an investment advisor. Kelly moved to Santa Fe and is doing well as a freelance photographer."

"When I first wrote you about the mural possibilities," Jackie said, "you were finishing a show of your work. How did that go?"

Kira leaned back in the soft leather chair next to the lighted fireplace that added welcome warmth to the evening and to their conversation. "When you and I were in school, I was mainly focused on painting and printmaking," Kira said. "Since then, my interests have expanded. The show had a wide range of my work: paintings and drawings of course, but also some ceramics and bronze sculpture."

She sat quietly for a moment before saying, "I figure, the wider the net, the greater the catch, so I try to offer a variety of pieces to attract buyers." She gave a short laugh. "I've even tried my hand at weaving. I haven't found much of a market for my rugs. They take up too much space on a gallery wall. But I keep trying different mediums. I never know what will sell."

"I had no idea your work was so diversified," Jackie said.

"I use the shotgun approach to my art and work in many art niches, rather than the rifle way, which is to concentrate on only one thing at a time. My work is harder to market because of the variety, but I seldom get bored."

Kira sipped the wine Warren had poured when they adjourned to the living room after dinner. "I was more than ready for a new project when you called. Your fifty-six-foot mural is quite a change from a thirty-six by forty-inch painting."

"I'm glad I contacted you," Jackie replied. "Each year we try to get a new artist to design for us. I thought you might enjoy the challenge."

"Indeed, I do. I like the idea of honoring those who have gone down with their ships. And I also like the thought of coming here and seeing you in your far-north setting. What a great place you've found!" Kira looked admiringly around the room and out the window at the now-darkened view that sparkled with lights from the town and the boats on the bay.

"Wait until we've had a chance to show you more of Raven Creek," Warren said. "We especially enjoy this time of year with the birches and alders turning gold and the fireweed bright red. Before you leave, we may even have some termination dust."

"What is that?" Kira asked. "It sounds like a fatal housekeeping problem."

Warren laughed and glanced down at Jackie, curled up beside him on the long sofa. "That's what we call the first snow of the season. It's a light dusting of snow high on the mountains, a warning that fall is coming to an end and winter waiting to appear. It is also a reminder to check the car tires, snow blower, and heating oil supply."

After listening a while longer, Warren excused himself to go to his office to work. Jackie and Kira reminisced for another forty-five minutes. Then, in spite of her best efforts to stay alert, Kira gave in to travel fatigue, said a sleepy "goodnight" and disappeared into the guest room. It contained a dresser, two drawers of which had been emptied for her use, an old rocking chair, many of Jackie's Alaskan animal paintings and, most importantly, two double beds with puffy comforters, which beckoned Kira to sample their warmth and softness. She'd intended to unpack before going to sleep, but instead, gave into temptation, dropped onto the bed nearest the door, and happily succumbed to its velvety comfort.

Chapter Five

Saturday

Kira looked out the window of her room the next morning and saw a clear sky and treetops steady against the blue. No wind, no rain. Perfect. Two hours later, with breakfast behind them, Warren ascended to his office, and Jackie and Kira drove to the Raven Creek Regional Train and Cruise Terminal, at the edge of town, where the music festival would be held and the mural painted.

Although Jackie had described the building to Kira, her words had been inadequate to convey the enormity of the structure. A vast, tan, metal-sided building, with three formidable double steel doors controlling access from the front, greeted them. It looked adequate to easily house several airplanes or all the passengers of the cruise ships it served. Gray concrete planters, solid and heavy enough to keep anything short of a tank from crashing through the entrance, were lined up in front of the building as if for defense. Summer flowers in the planters had long since succumbed to the threat of approaching winter. Their dried, twisted stems topped by withered blossoms did nothing to make the entrance appealing and gave clear notice that the cruise season was a thing of the past.

When the last passengers departed for destinations farther south, the cruise line company willingly made the building available for community use. However, Jackie told Kira, the company made clear to all the groups using the building that they expected it to be left undamaged and definitely without paint splatters on the floor or in the restrooms. It was in this mammoth structure that the mural would be painted.

They parked in the large empty lot and walked to the building, where Jackie unlocked the doors and swung one open. They entered an enormous dark and echoing space. Kira immediately felt like an intruder in a great cavern and imagined she could hear the vast interior breathing out silence. The still air was an unexpected contrast to the living breeze outside the heavy metal doors.

Seeming immune to Kira's fantasies, Jackie turned on the lights in the front half of the building and began explaining the activities Kira could expect to see this first day of work.

Her list of "to dos" seemed endless. She explained that there would be four days of preparatory work. The painting itself would be completed during the music festival, from Friday night to Sunday afternoon. Fifteen percent of the floor space had been allotted for mural activities, the remainder was divided among entertainment acts, food, craft sales, and a children's play area.

Kira learned the mural volunteers would first spread and tape plastic sheeting in place to protect the floor from falling paint, then set up tables for the four-by-eight-foot panels to rest on while being painted. Hauling in paint and other supplies would depend on need and the opportunity to get them out of storage.

Jackie explained that while their work area was being prepared, another space would be used for sanding the twenty-eight aluminum panels that would make up the total mural when assembled. They were heavy and awkward to move—the edges sharp and dangerous to hold if not handled carefully (thick gloves recommended). Their flexibility made positioning them a two-person job.

She described the arrival, three days earlier, of the panels in large, plastic-wrapped bundles. Now she looked with apparent pleasure on their bulk, saying their presence meant she wouldn't have to frantically contact the trucking company to locate them, as she had one year when the shipment didn't arrived on time.

"In the past we used exterior grade plywood but, even with lots of primer, they didn't hold up to the weather," Jackie said. "After a few years outside they had to be taken down and repainted. Redoing a previous year's mural, as well as producing a new one, was almost too much to do in one week." She touched the white sheets of metal. "So we searched and researched other supporting materials. These seem to be the answer—at least if we do the preparation correctly." She moved her hand gently over a stack. "The first year we didn't do it properly, and the paint began peeling almost as soon as the mural was installed outdoors. We contacted the manufacturer of the panels, as well as the paint company. They both told us we should have sanded that beautiful smooth surface before priming it. We had to repaint all of them."

Jackie introduced Kira to the volunteers as they arrived. All were dressed in work pants, sweaters, sweatshirts, or various styles of jackets. The first to arrive was Owen Martin, the owner of the missing *Halibut Hunter*. In his forties, with his blond hair slightly receding and his waistline moderately expanding, he was still a handsome man. Kira found his cheerful, outgoing personality attractive. "Looks as though we have a great day to begin work," he said to Jackie, his white teeth contrasting brightly with his tanned skin when he smiled.

He turned to Kira. "Welcome to Alaska. I must tell you how impressed we all were with your mural design. We were amazed by how you combined all the different sinking occasions into one painting. I hadn't thought it could be done. It will make a wonderful addition to our community."

As an artist, Kira was always pleased by praise of her work. This time was no exception. *I think I'm going to like working with this man.*

Owen obviously intended to enjoy being a part of the workforce. "I've participated in painting several of these murals," he continued. "Now I'll be in from the start. In fact, Jackie asked me to be 'in charge' of the paint table this year. I'm not exactly sure what it will entail. However, I know she'll enlighten me." He turned his broad face toward Jackie and winked.

"It's a big, sometimes messy, job, but I'm confident Owen can handle it," Jackie mocked. They were obviously old friends and comfortable with teasing each other.

Owen nodded, then saying he'd better get to work before he was thrown out, turned toward the pile of large sheets of plastic. Picking up a few, he asked where they would be working this year. Snatching up a roll of duct tape, he walked to the area indicated by Jackie.

"He's very active here in town," Jackie told Kira, as they walked to the wrapped stack of panels. "Chamber of Commerce, investor, businessman, and general community supporter. In addition to having an office here in town, he owns the boatyard across the bay. You can see it from my office at home. They store, repair, and launch boats. It never seems busy when I drive over, but it's an interesting place. Some of the local teenagers have been hanging around there for years. In fact, Vin, the son of Jason Tiedemann, the captain who died, is one of that group. I've always felt Owen was an especially kind and patient man to let those boys run free out there. I'm glad he's able to take this week off to help us."

"He's certainly a good-looking man." Kira watched with interest as he began to spread the plastic sheeting on the floor. "Does he have a family?" She reminded herself, *I'm here to paint. I don't need to get involved with a man living in Alaska, of all places.*

"Unfortunately for him, no," Jackie replied. "His wife died in a car accident several years ago when she was in California visiting her parents. They had no children. Since her death, he has gone out casually with a few women. I suppose he just hasn't found the right person. It's too bad. I like him."

So do I, Kira thought.

The next people to arrive were Angela Tiedemann, daughter of the man found dead in the bay, and Kelly Singleton. At first Kira was surprised to learn the girl would be helping, even in these early steps of preparation. However, after some thought, Angela's presence made sense. Her father's boat was to be one of those depicted. She would naturally want to be involved from the beginning.

Angela looked to be seventeen or eighteen, small but sturdily-built, with long dark hair tied back. She seemed very quiet and reserved, as though still burdened by the loss of her father and the growing speculation as to his possible activities. Her dark eyes were solemn when she greeted everyone.

Kelly was about twenty, average height, slender, but well-muscled. Kira thought that he was the kind of man any girl might be attracted to. Later, she noticed that, even when he was busy unfolding and taping down the plastic sheets to cover the floor, he appeared to keep a protective watch on Angela as she met the others who came to work.

Jackie had mentioned that Kelly wanted to marry Angela, but for some reason she was dragging her feet. "You'd think her unhappiness about her dad would make Angela turn toward Kelly. It hasn't had that effect. People are asking why, and beginning to wonder if she thinks Kelly might have had some involvement in her father's trouble and disappearance. I can't imagine Kelly doing that, but rumors have started. They always do."

The doorway temporarily darkened as two more people came in. Jackie introduced the first one as Donald Lansing. "Donald teaches in our high school—English to unbelievers. His unwilling students are convinced 'texting' is our new official language." Jackie laughed, patting his arm. "I think his is a lost cause, but he perseveres. Don is one of the last links with civilization as our generation knew it."

"It's not quite that bad," Don replied good-naturedly, tucking his wire-rimed glasses into his battered suede jacket. "Most are good kids, just too impatient, wanting to do things their own way."

Nathan Barnes, who accompanied Don, spoke up. "He certainly opened my eyes to grammar when I took his class. I ain't done nothin' but talk English good since he learned me."

They all laughed. Nathan's face was freckled. His unruly red hair and moustache, combined with his confident stance, proclaimed his outgoing personality. He looked as though he would get along with everyone he met. With a theatrical grimace he asked Jackie, "Now, what heavy lifting have you planned for us today?"

Jackie and the two men were immediately immersed in a discussion about the positioning of tables, panels, and sanding equipment.

Later that morning, Angela and Kira labored together to remove the plastic film that protected each side of the aluminum panels. "We pull the film off one side only." Angela explained. "We keep the second protected, just in case something goes wrong with the paint or there is damage to the panel itself. Then we can turn it over and start again." She stopped to stretch her back and relax her fingers from the strain of griping the plastic. "They are too expensive to just throw away."

"Have you worked on many of these murals?" Kira asked, as they again bent to their task.

"Oh, yes. But this is the one I have been anticipating . . . and dreading," Angela added softly.

Kira gave her a sympathetic glance before asking, "Because of your father's boat being included?"

Angela nodded. Her eyes seemed to glaze over, as she looked away and gazed into space for a moment.

Kira said, "Jackie told me what happened. I can only imagine how difficult it is for you. Perhaps the painting will become an act of love and offer some consolation for his loss."

Angela shrugged and, considering for a moment, said, "It might be some consolation if people would just stop making up stories. My father was a good man! He spent many hours taking sportsmen out fishing to support us. I'll admit Vin and I didn't always get along with him. He was sort of distant with us and was out on the *Halibut Hunter* a lot. Still, I can't believe all these stories about him doing something bad. I just won't!" She turned away abruptly and seemed to be searching for someone.

Kelly looked up from where he was working, smiled and walked to where she was standing. "How about a break for lunch?" he asked, putting his hand on Angela's shoulder. "I don't know about you, but I'm cold and my knees are sore from crawling on the cement to tape all that plastic in place."

Angela produced a weak smile in assent. As she moved to accompany Kelly out to his pickup, she said over her shoulder to Kira, "Even if my father did do something wrong—and I don't know why he would—his boat still deserves to be in the painting."

CHAPTER SIX

Vin drove into the boatyard about seven-fifteen in the evening. When he saw his friends' cars parked near the office, he knew he was the last to arrive. The young men had known each other all through school and used the boatyard as a meeting hangout since they were old enough to ride their bikes so far out of town.

He noticed the light was beginning to fade. The season was changing, although at Raven Creek's latitude, daylight still lingered into the later hours. The long days of summer confused the tourists who couldn't understand why the stores closed so early. "For heaven's sake," they would grumble. "It's still light out." Only after they checked their watches would they realize it was nine-thirty or ten o'clock at night, and they were the ones out of synch.

He parked his car in front of a large, weathered building, which held the offices of Owen Martin and some of his shipyard employees. It also provided an indoor workspace, meeting room, and lounge for the workers. Scattered about the property, in old outbuildings that hadn't seen paint or much attention for years, were storage areas for seldom-used tools and other equipment and supplies.

Vin gazed at dispirited-looking boats of every description, age, and condition, propped up on heavy timbers at the side and back of the workshop. Weeds grew high around the old boats, which looked for the most part like abandoned wrecks collected by a playful giant after a thunderous storm and placed in straggling rows to await further attention. If any restoration or repairs were in progress, they were minimal at best.

A wheeled boatlift for moving boats in or out of the water waited on a cracked cement pad near the water. Weeds surrounded it, though they were shorter than those engulfing the destitute boats in back. Vin figured the lift had seen only limited use during the summer.

Owen, the owner of the facility, and of the boat Vin's dad skippered, always welcomed the boys, insisting only that they not mess with any tools in the storage sheds while playing their interminable games or treasure hunting. Vin remembered the times, when the weather made being outside unpleasant, that Owen had told stories of the old boats stored in the yard, indulging the boy's appetites for adventure. Of course, some stories were outrageously improbable, but he was a good storyteller, so they easily forgave his exaggerations.

Vin let himself into the slightly dilapidated and unlighted building, from which the day-workers had already departed. As he walked across the gloomy shop, his steps echoed under the high roof whose beams disappeared into the darkness. He heard the voices of his friends coming from the lounge, and made out Tory's muted voice saying, "And he didn't even benefit from . . ." and then a laugh.

As Vin opened the door Mike was saying, "Now, that's not . . ." He stopped speaking when Vin entered. Then in a somewhat overly hearty voice said, "Good to see you. It's about time you came. Have a beer. I liberated some from the fridge at home." Mike pointed to a table in a shadowed corner.

Mike and Vin had shared homework, secrets, and adventures since they first met and found they were kindred spirits. Both hoped to attend the local technical college: Mike in culinary arts, with plans to eventually own his own restaurant, Vin in computer programming. Mike would begin classes in the fall. Vin's computer dreams remained just that—dreams. His father had said he would have to wait until the fishing season was over before they could talk about classes. Until then, Vin had better be looking for a job. After a half-hearted search, he'd managed to find temporary work. Now his dad was dead. Vin didn't know what to do.

"Thanks," Vin said, walking across the dusty cement floor to the beat-up metal picnic table that held the cans. He realized that all talk had suddenly ceased with his entrance. He looked around inquiringly, wondering what he'd interrupted.

Seeming aware of the sudden silence, Mike spoke quickly. "We were tossing around ideas for this mural the town is talking about." He stopped, apparently realizing the direction the conversation would inevitably take.

"Yeah, my sister started working on it today," Vin said, purposely showing no sign of the discomfort the others seemed to expect from him.

Two of his friends, Eagle and Dodger, sat quietly in a far corner. Eagle worked in the fish-processing plant in Raven Creek. It was hard, repetitive labor, but seemed to satisfy him. Although the pay was good, he never showed evidence of his increased income, unless it was in the quantity of beer he had available. He was a skinny, unhealthy-looking guy and could be relied upon to show up late whenever the six guys planned special activities. Vin would have been surprised if Eagle managed to get to work on time, and marveled that he kept his job.

Eagle hung with Dodger, whose parents had divorced five years before. Dodger insisted he didn't mind or miss his father very much, but he had become quieter and his grades had plummeted. With his six-foot-three height and bright red hair, he was easy to find in a crowd. This summer he had found work at the Premium Pizza Palace.

Dodger said, "I saw Angela at the Palace yesterday with Kelly. They were taking a break, I guess. She was awfully quiet."

"I suppose she was thinking about Dad," Vin said. "She isn't satisfied with the police and Coast Guard reports."

Eagle spoke up, saying, "Does she still believe there was more to his death than the reports mentioned?"

Sliding onto the metal picnic table bench, Vin said, "Well, they were inconclusive. We can't understand why he had a bullet wound. He wasn't the type to shoot himself. It's frustrating, but there's nothing we can do but wait and see if anything new turns up."

Tory, the first speaker Vin had heard as he came in, was wearing his usual self-righteous expression. His youthful rashness had recently grown into an overconfident, bullying manner. Vin thought he now spoke as though his ideas and opinions were the best informed and the most important of all. Of medium height and hefty build, with tousled black hair and dark challenging eyes, he walked with a swagger that was daily becoming more pronounced. Vin often wondered what could have brought on this change. He didn't think it was due only to his drinking, although that was increasing lately. Whatever it was, Vin found his biting comments increasingly difficult to ignore.

"Yeah. I hear your old man's causing a fuss among the 'up-tights.' " Tory smirked. "They say he was out to make some extra cash 'cause of your step-mom. She's sure been dressing hot these days." Tory laughed loudly and looked at the others as though to make sure they appreciated his wit.

"That's going too far, Tory, and you know it," Mike broke in. He seemed aware of his friend's sensitivity on the subject of the stepmother he neither wanted nor liked.

"Aw, come on, Tory," Helmond said. "Selena came from Anchorage. She must be bored with his dad gone so much. You can't blame her for wanting to dress up and have a good time." He seemed to be thinking deeply. "Of course, that Reynaldo pal of hers is a mighty sly dude." He giggled.

As Tory had become more aggressive over time, his friend Helmond's personality appeared to weaken. Though Helmond's words sometimes seemed unthinking, Vin thought he was not really unkind, but simply unaware of the impact on others of what he said. Already stoop shouldered, Helmond seemed to have grown too fast for his muscles to support his height. His curly hair was long and combed forward, partially covering his face. In effect, he had grown his own hiding place. A beer drinker since he was first able to con someone into buying it for him, he had recently begun using drugs. Now their use was starting to show.

His mood swings were becoming more severe, his other-world expression more noticeable.

Vin looked up abruptly at Helmond's comment. "Reynaldo? What's he got to do with anything? Dad barely knew him."

Tory leered. "Your dad may not have known him very well, but your stepmother sure does."

Rising from the bench, Vin strode over to face Tory. "That's a vicious thing to say about Selena," he said, his voice rising. "You don't know what the hell you're talking about." Vin shook with anger. "God knows she's not my favorite person, but I won't listen to crap like that. Take it back or come outside. Nobody says that without paying for it." His fists were clenched. The beer forgotten.

Getting up, Mike walked rapidly to where Tory sat at ease. Next to him, Helmond looked as though he didn't understand what was making Vin so mad. "Tory, what's got into you? We're all supposed to be friends." Mike's obvious puzzlement was mixed with anger at the provocation.

Tory shrugged. "I'm getting sick of Vin sticking his head in the sand. Everyone knows what's going on between those two, so what's the big deal?" Tory sipped his drink, then leaned back as though to watch an entertaining show.

Putting a hand on Vin's arm, Mike urged him away. "Forget it, Vin. Tory has had one too many beers." With a warning glare at Tory, he added, "He doesn't know anything. He's just trying to make you mad."

"Well, he did that," Vin grumbled. Raising his voice, he added, "You don't know when to shut up, Tory. Your mouth is going to get you in trouble one day."

"Yeah, yeah," Tory said under his breath, as Mike and Vin turned to join Dodger and Eagle, who now sprawled in battered, gray plastic chairs next to a cold electric heater. Behind him, Vin heard Tory say to Helmond, "He don't like to hear the truth, but his step-mom's been running around. Nothing Vin says is going to change that. His dad wasn't lily white either."

Vin turned toward the two in time to see Helmond smirk and nod. "You're right, man. You're always right."

"Like hell he's right! I didn't always get along with Dad," Vin growled, "but he wouldn't do something illegal. He was straight."

"Straight can start to bend when money is tight. Everyone knows your step-mom's on a constant spending spree."

Vin was too angry to talk. He knew money had been in short supply recently. He'd heard his dad arguing with Selena about her bills. But would his father really do something illegal? No! His dad was a pain in the ass sometimes, but Vin couldn't believe what Tory was saying. And the "talk of the town." What did these idiots know?

Vin looked around the room at the guys he'd once thought his friends. Their relationships were changing, and he wasn't ready for it. It was clear that Tory and Helmond were lost as pals. Dodger and Eagle were still friends, but Vin could feel himself growing beyond them. They seemed to have no definite plans or dreams for their futures. They just wanted to get by. Mike was the only one Vin could still count on.

All right. He would show them. There had to be a way to find out what really happened to his father. Someone must have hijacked his boat. How else could the gunshot wound be explained? His dad was too tough to be suicidal, too stubborn to be a quitter, too honest to be a smuggler.

After their father disappeared, Vin and Angela had hoped Selena would just take off and leave them alone. She had done nothing but complain since she and Jason married. She wanted new clothes, entertainment, and travel, such as a winter in Hawaii, where many of the captains went at the end of the summer fishing season in Raven Creek. She couldn't convince Jason to leave. Vin and Angela were still in school, and Jason wanted them to stay in town with their friends. It was Vin's opinion that his father should never have married Selena. Nothing was good enough for her. *My God! What had she expected? Did she think a sport fishing boat made enough money for all she wanted?*

It was too late now. His father was dead, that family conflict a thing of the past. However, if Selena had a hand in his father's death, he would find out. *She would regret it.*

CHAPTER SEVEN

Sunday

Sunday was a non-workday, so Jackie and Warren invited Kira to lunch at Evan's Fish House down at the small boat harbor. They assured her that, as this was Alaska, no formal attire was expected, although clean and neat were appreciated. Most visitors were able to adhere to this standard, most of the time. Several outstanding restaurants were located on the dock, but a meal at Evan's was considered a "must." It was open only during the summer months. Late in the season, when the tourist trade slowed, the locals returned in greater numbers to eat in "their restaurant." Before closing, Evan's would have a one-day, half-price blowout to empty the freezers. Then the owner would lock the doors and not reopen until spring.

The three were being shown to a table by windows with a spectacular view of the harbor and sunlit mountains across the bay, when Jackie stopped to talk to a couple at a nearby table. Warren explained to Kira that those were the owners of the building where the finished mural would be mounted.

The Manowins, Frank and Sharon, invited the three to join them. The waiter brought extra chairs and the group was soon seated. As a visitor, Kira was given the seat with the best view of the harbor. The first thing she noticed was the swinging confusion of masts. The dock looked alive with them. To the right a tour boat was offloading its passengers. Frank explained that after setting the boat to rights from the first tour, the crew would reload for the afternoon viewing. He said that in the summer their passenger loads were greater than those this late in the season, when the tourists were beginning to go home. Even now, to Kira's eyes, there seemed enough people waiting to board to make the trips pay. When she asked about the sport fishing boats, Frank said it was too early in the day for them to be returning.

"We are so happy to meet you," Sharon gushed. "Frank and I admired your design and wondered what you would be like. We want to hear all about you." With a bright smile she looked around the group at the table.

Her husband nodded his assent. The cool northern light from the windows glinted on his glasses as he spoke. "Your work will be on our building for years to come, a most welcome addition to our store and to Raven Creek."

Sharon hastened to inform Kira that, upon learning the subject of this year's mural, the Manowins had campaigned to have it installed on the side of their building. Their marine supply store in the old part of town had a long blank wall facing a busy secondary street. The mural committee had pronounced it an excellent location. Now they were eager to ask questions about Kira's work, especially the research that had gone into the design of the image. They'd had no say in the design—that was between the artist and the committee—but they assured everyone they'd been very pleased when shown the final, approved plans.

Frank asked, "Have you designed many murals?"

"Over my career I've done many paintings, but this is first mural I was ever asked to create," Kira admitted. "Now, after all my research, I feel right at home in Raven Creek." She added, "Although, after reading of the storms you have around here, I'm definitely not inclined to go boating on my own."

"They can be pretty fearsome if you aren't prepared." Frank laughed, running his hand through his thinning gray hair. With his arm raised, his brown and white pinstriped shirt barely covered the bulge of his stomach. "Of course, those storms help keep us in business. Knowing the dangers out there, skippers tend to keep their equipment repaired, or better yet, replaced."

When the drinks and menus arrived, the talk turned to what they would order. Sharon assured Kira the fish was fresh, right off the boats that docked in the harbor each afternoon. "I like the salmon best, but the halibut is outstanding, too. After lunch we'll be able to watch some of the fishing boats come into the harbor. Wait until you see the size of those halibut! They're enormous! Some weigh over three hundred pounds."

The woman sounded serious about the heavy weight, but it all seemed like a "fish story" to Kira. She was willing to go along with the joke, so she asked, "How do they get them up to the cleaning area? They must need a forklift for fish that size."

"They wheel them up in those sturdy gray wheelbarrows parked over there." Sharon gestured toward the top of the ramp running down to the boat dock. "The halibut are so big and slippery that it often takes two people to load and move them."

Her disbelief must have been obvious, although Kira was trying to hide it. Frank pointed to a thick, telephone pole-sized log that was placed across the top of two large vertical posts. It was festooned with pulleys and two rows of hooks. "The first thing the fishermen do is hoist their entire catch onto that log construction over there. Then they stand or kneel in front of all the dead fish to have their pictures taken. The 'great hunter' syndrome."

"Will we see any halibut today? I simply can't imagine fish that large," Kira said.

"You'll see halibut. The three hundred pounders aren't that common anymore, but the ones they catch almost every day still are very large."

Gazing at the log construction, Kira noticed what looked like whiskers on the top crossbar. "What are those spike things sticking up from the beam?"

Sharon answered, "Seagulls are always hungry and on the prowl for a scraps. Without those prickly wires they might swarm the fish display, and poop on the catch and fishermen. The wires discourage their attentions."

Frank continued explaining the process. "After all the photos are taken, the fish go back into the wheelbarrows and are moved to the gutting tables. The cleaning is very fast. After a day on the water, the captains have no desire to linger on the job. The proud clients and their friends usually stand nearby to watch them work."

"The knives used are extremely sharp," Warren said. "The halibut cheeks are prime cuts. To get the other meat they remove the backbone and fins, but have to be careful where they cut. Since halibut are bottom feeders, they are full of worms. Cut the wrong place and the meat is ruined."

"Yuck. I'm not sure I wanted to know that," Kira said with a grimace.

"That's why the skipper does the cleaning. An amateur could ruin the entire day's catch." Warren paused a moment, then added, "After the fish are cleaned, the meat is stored in coolers to be taken home or sent to a local company for freezing or drying before shipping."

After gazing at the work area for a few minutes, Kira commented, "It looks very tidy after all that cutting has gone on. Does the town have a cleanup crew?"

"No. The skippers do their own cleanup," Jackie said. "They use those hoses hanging there to rinse off their tables and the fish. Can you make out the slot between the two long tables? There are vertical boards on each side."

Kira leaned toward Sharon's chair to see more clearly. "It's hard to make out. What are they for?"

"We can show you later. It's the slot where all the unwanted parts of the fish are dropped into the gut barge below. When the barge is full, people from the harbormaster's office tow it across the bay and empty it. They have to wear rain gear and hats— seagulls again."

"I think I'll have salmon," Kira declared. "Somehow the halibut has lost its allure."

"You'll change your mind once you taste some." Jackie laughed as the waiter arrived to take their orders.

Over lunch the talk was about fishing, the economy, the mural, and local politics. There was some discussion about the *Halibut Hunter* and what might have happened to it, its captain, and crewman. No one seemed to know anything definite, but theories were abundant. The Manowins were moderately concerned about the controversy, and wondered if having the mural on their building would affect their business negatively. In spite of their uncertainty, they sounded willing to go along with any decision the mural society might make. Jackie assured them there would be no problems.

"I don't see that one boat more or less will matter in the final design," Frank said. "Is keeping that one boat in the painting worth all the fuss?"

"Its inclusion may cause some talk, but it was based here in Raven Creek," Jackie reminded him, "and we shouldn't forget the feelings of Vin and Angela. Their dad was all the support they really had." Jackie spoke solemnly. "Their stepmother, Selena, has shown little interest in their lives. I think she was disappointed by the lack of social life here. You know, don't you, that Angela is helping with the mural? I watched her working on the panels yesterday. Sometimes she seemed sad. Other times she had a little smile on her face when she was looking at Kira's drawing that I'd posted on the wall."

Even though Angela had said very little about her feelings, Jackie and Kira agreed the project was very important to the girl's ability to come to terms with the loss of her father. She was taking part in creating a memorial for him and others who had been lost at sea. She needed the community's acknowledgment of his value, as well as their acceptance of his worthiness to be commemorated, gunshot or no gunshot.

"Speak of the devil." Warren commented. "Look over there. Isn't that Selena, Angela's infamous step-mom, sitting at a table with what I think the kids would once have labeled a 'cool' guy?"

Sharon slowly turned her head. "Good heavens! That's Reynaldo Lovato," she sputtered. "He works for Owen," she told Kira. "Perhaps she met him through Jason, although I don't know how." Sharon returned her gaze to those at her table and asked, "I wonder what Selena is doing here—and with him?"

"I think that's obvious," Warren observed cynically. "Now that Jason's dead, she's not wasting time finding someone else to pay her bills."

"I've met him," Frank said. After a quick look at the two he turned back. "I don't want to be noticed staring." He continued in a confidential tone, "I must say, he doesn't strike me as the kind to get involved with a cash drain like Selena. He's a bookkeeper for Owen Martin and a few other people. I'd expect him to be careful about his money."

"She's very good looking. That could be enough reason," Warren suggested.

"You men are so bad," Jackie said. "Why shouldn't she spend time with a friend of Jason's?" She paused, and then added, "Although this one wouldn't be my first choice."

They watched Selena lean close to Reynaldo to whisper. It was Kira's opinion that his expression was not that of a lover, more of a conspirator. He sported chin whiskers, rimless glasses, and an abundance of light brown, rather long, hair. His clothes appeared of good quality, but slightly theatrical and out of place on him. He frowned at Selena and shook his head. Selena appeared to redouble her efforts, putting her hand over his. He continued to look down at his glass as though he could somehow ignore her talk if he focused hard enough on the remaining liquid and melting ice. Finally, after she had spoken intently for a few moments more, he looked up, resignation in his narrow face, and nodded slowly.

Leaning back in obvious satisfaction, Selena suddenly became aware of their audience. Abruptly collecting her belongings and taking a last swallow of her drink, she arose and stalked out. Reynaldo raised a thin hand, motioning to the waiter for the bill. After paying, he seized his black leather jacket from the back of his chair and walked rapidly out of the room.

The five at the table looked wonderingly at each other. "What was that all about?" asked Sharon.

Kira was curious about the rapid breakup and Selena's abnormally abrupt disappearance. Certainly not the ending a casual meeting would produce. Was something more questionable going on here than friends showing bad judgment so soon after the death of one of their partners?

CHAPTER EIGHT

Monday

Don Lansing and Owen Martin were already in the terminal building when Jackie and Kira arrived. The men had rinsed off the dust remaining on the panels from Saturday's sanding and moved them onto the painting tables to dry. As Don and Owen positioned two more panels to be sanded, they turned to greet the newcomers. "We're relieved to see you weren't expecting us to do all the work today," Don teased. "I was going to suggest to Owen that we break for an early coffee if you didn't show up soon."

"Don, don't even consider slipping out early." Jackie laughed, with mock threat. "You've only begun to work. When Angela comes, she and Kira can begin sanding again. Until then, use your energy to paint those panels you just cleaned. Owen probably has the primer stashed somewhere on the paint table. After he finds the cans," Jackie said, grinning. "Those panels will need two coats before the mural colors go on."

She walked toward the long table at the side of the room that held cans of paint, water containers, foam brushes, rollers, and other assorted painting equipment. "I know Warren brought over some primer Saturday . . . now where . . . ? Oh, there it is. Don, if you will get that paint pan and roller, you can start putting on the first coat. Remember to do the edges too."

"Yes, sir." He gave a mock salute.

While Jackie and Don searched for a can opener and stirring sticks, Owen wandered back to the sanding area, where Kira had just shed her jacket. "Let me help," he offered, coming up behind her as she was trying to tie her apron. "After all my years working with boats, I should be able to tie a decent bow."

"Thank you," Kira accepted readily. "My fingers are a little clumsy this morning. I'm not used to your chilly weather."

"If you stay here long, you will come to like it. Our winters are quite mild compared to what they get in Fairbanks. Up there, the university has built tunnels to connect the various buildings, so the students don't have to go out in the minus-too-many-degrees cold."

Kira cringed, imagining the discomfort temperatures that low would produce. "The weather here may seem almost tropical in comparison, but it's the long hours of winter darkness I'd have trouble living with. I'd want to hibernate with the bears until spring."

"Oh, no," Owen assured her. "No one has to hide inside all winter. We have lots of things to do. With the tourists mostly gone, many stores closed, and the fishing halted, our town's social life becomes very active. You'll see if you decide to stay here. I expect you'd enjoy it."

Kira thought she detected an invitation in his voice but had no intention of saying more on the subject—at least not now.

At that moment, Angela and Kelly pushed through the front doors. Angela seemed more relaxed today, and called out, "Hello, all."

Kira thanked Owen for his help, then strolled over to Angela. "I'm glad you're here. I didn't want to face all this sanding by myself. Now, with two of us working, we should easily finish today."

While Angela put on an apron to protect her clothes from the sanding dust, Kelly sauntered to the pile of untouched panels. He grinned as he spoke to Owen. "I guess we're the ones who'll be unwrapping the remaining panels and hauling them from one table to the next."

Owen ruefully agreed with this, and went to help hold a panel upright while Kelly pulled the protective film from one side. By the time they finished peeling a couple of boards, Angela and Kira had completed sanding the one they were working on. The men carried the sanded one outside for a rinse with the hose. After drying it, they transferred it to the painting area. Meanwhile, it was replaced with a fresh panel, and the sanding began again.

Angela stood on one side of the panel, Kira on the other, but not directly across from each other. They wanted to avoid colliding as they circled their sanders on the board. The finish was thin, so it was necessary to concentrate on what they were doing. When the gray of the aluminum began to show, it was time to move to another area.

The electric palm sanders were too loud to allow conversation. Talk was possible only when they were turned off for new panels to be put in place. During one of the breaks, Kira straightened slowly, groaning a little from stiffness. As she brushed the sanded powdered paint from her sleeves and removed her dust mask she said, "You seem to be feeling better today, Angela. Did you have a restful weekend?"

Angela leaned back to stretch. "Oh, yes. Kelly and I walked on the beach and watched the eagles, gulls, and sea otters. It was very relaxing. We sat on logs washed up on the gravel and talked about all sorts of things. He convinced me I should just ignore the smuggling rumors. Because that's all they are . . . rumors."

"He's right. It's a waste of your energy to pay attention to stories invented by ignorant people who don't know the facts. Besides, no one knows, or may ever know, what happened."

Angela shook the dust from her apron. "We talked about my father, too. I wasn't close to him—he was often away fishing—but I still loved him. Recently, he seemed distracted, more remote. I've always thought his marriage to Selena was a mistake. I frequently heard them arguing about her bills, and I know she was becoming bored and unhappy living here. I don't know what she had expected, but . . ." She didn't finish the sentence.

Hoping to take advantage of this new openness from Angela, Kira said, "I saw Selena at Evan's Fish House yesterday."

Angela glanced up quickly. "I can't imagine her eating there alone. Who was she with?"

"Reynaldo Lovato. Do you know him?"

"Oh, him," she said dismissively. "He works for Owen. I suppose he could be interested in her. If she ever thought of him as more than just a friend, she hid it well. At least she did while Dad was alive."

When Owen and Kelly came over, the women stepped back from the table so the boards could be exchanged. Then it was sanding time again and an end to conversation.

Angela must have been turning their words over in her mind, Kira thought, because later that morning, she again brought up the subject of Reynaldo. "I wonder if Selena thinks he has a lot of money. That might explain her interest in him." Thoughtfully, she added, "I've wondered about him. He does dress well. That would appeal to her. But where does his money come from?" She hesitated. "Could it be connected with drugs in some way?"

Startled at this turn in the conversation, Kira asked, "What made you think of that? I suppose it's possible, but Raven Creek seems like such a quiet, peaceful town." Then she reconsidered. *But drugs can find their way to almost any place these days. Jackie had said her first husband was distributing them.*

After a pause, Angela explained that drugs were definitely a problem in Raven Creek, though many people didn't realize it yet. Some of the kids from the "best" families attended parties where drugs were easily available. Their parents were not aware of what was going on, and probably wouldn't believe it of their children if they were told. "Vin thinks some of his friends are involved. He hasn't said much, but he's noticed changes in some of the guys he grew up with. He doesn't know their drug source yet."

"Yet?"

"He worries that a couple of them, Troy and Helmut, might be more than a little involved, perhaps distributing or something. But he has no proof."

"Has he said if he suspects anyone else?" Kira found this conversation eye-opening.

Angela said quietly, "We've sometimes wondered where Selena was getting her drugs. We know she was using. Vin and I found some in the house one day. Do you think . . . I mean . . . I know it's unlikely . . . but could Reynaldo be the one who got them for her? She's been seen with him more often since Dad died." She shook her head, seeming confused.

As they continued to talk, Angela admitted she didn't know Reynaldo well. He had been around town for several years, and she had not heard anything negative about him. He seemed a quiet person, lived by himself in a nice condo overlooking the bay, and worked as a bookkeeper for Owen and other business people. "This is all so muddled. I don't like suspecting people," Angela finally said.

That was the end of the conversation, but several times Kira noticed a bewildered frown on Angela's face. It was obvious she felt growing concern about the situation. Kira thought it unfair that Angela should be worrying about Selena and drugs, in addition to her father's mysterious death.

CHAPTER NINE

In the house she'd shared with Jason, Selena untangled herself from the sheets that had wrapped themselves around her as she'd tossed restlessly in her sleep. She slipped out of bed and pulled on her robe. Nothing seemed to be working out as she had hoped. Although Reynaldo was usually willing to cater to her desire for good times, either by entertaining her with meals at suitably secluded restaurants, driving her to Anchorage, or renewing her supply of drugs, he had so far shown little inclination to engage in a long-lasting marital commitment. A girl had to look out for the future, and without a commitment, there was less guarantee of income—hell, there was no guarantee.

Without Jason's body, Selena had been unable to get her hands on any insurance money. Now that his body had been found, she expected her life to get better, although not as much, or as soon, as she'd hoped. Debts would have to be paid. To live the life she wanted, she needed much more than the insurance would bring— and that might have to be shared with the kids if they realized how much of it was theirs. Free of constraints, but without money, she'd be even worse off than before. So the question arose, how could she solve her problems and find more cash?

She had counted on Jason making plenty of money from his charter fishing—what a fool she had been—and look where she was now, facing an uncertain future and stuck in the role of stepmother to two ungrateful kids. She'd let them think almost all of Jason's money came to her. Thank God they hadn't paid attention at the reading of the will. Most of what little money Jason had left went to those two brats. She received a limited income, and that for only two years. Time was passing much too swiftly and her financial future was still up in the air. It was time to look around for other sources of income.

Glancing out from her bedroom window a short time later, Selena saw Owen Martin walk past the colorful crab-trap floats Jason had collected and hung from a tree by the gate. He came carefully along the broken sidewalk toward the door. She let him ring the bell several times before finally opening the door. It wouldn't do to seem too eager to see him. He was dressed in jeans and a multicolored flannel shirt. *He's probably going to help at the terminal. He's a handsome man with his light blue eyes and usually laughing mouth.* Even though he owned the boat Jason skippered, she had met him infrequently before Jason's disappearance. After Jason's death he'd helped her with the paperwork and legal issues surrounding the disappearance and then the discovery of the body.

Her voice low and welcoming, Selena said, "Come in, Owen. I slept late today and was just about to get dressed." She pulled her robe tightly about her body. "How nice of you to come over. Can I get you a drink, orange juice, coffee, something stronger?" She backed away so he could enter the dark front room. She was always slightly embarrassed when visitors came. The room was neat enough, but nothing could disguise the age of the furniture. She'd bought a few new pieces before Jason rebelled at the costs, but the house still needed a lot of work before she could be proud of it. Now, with Jason gone and no money coming in, the house would have to remain as it was.

"No thanks, Selena." He seated himself in an overstuffed leather armchair with a sagging seat. It had been Jason's favorite, although Selena couldn't imagine why. It looked old enough to have been in the house since it was built. "I just stopped by to see how you're doing. I've been thinking about you recently, wondering if there was any other way I can help."

Selena glanced up at him thoughtfully. She knew her gray eyes were among her best features and she was practiced at putting them to good use. In her softest voice she said, "How sweet of you. I'd be all right if the police could give me some definite answers." Exhibiting a distressed frown and releasing a tear, she said, "If you will excuse me, I'll just get something to drink from the kitchen and be right back. It's still early for me."

While Jason's boat and whereabouts had been unknown, Selena lived in fear he might have been angered by her bills and simply walked out. She had frantically considered what options she had if he were gone for good. She hated living trapped in this nowhere burg. Leaving town for shopping in Anchorage helped. Her dream was that someday she'd be shopping in New York or Paris—that would really be living. She called from the kitchen, "Are you sure I can't get you anything? The coffee is already brewed and hot."

"No thanks. I'll have plenty of caffeine by the end of today. That's one thing in great supply at the terminal."

Selena did a quick check of her appearance in the mirror by the back door. Earlier, when brushing her mass of curly auburn hair, she'd smiled with satisfaction, knowing that she had maintained her figure and hadn't lost her looks. In fact, she'd thought, she looked sexier than ever.

She had been grateful for Owen's help with the funeral arrangements after the police finished with the body. That had been a confusing time. She'd not dared to accept the suicide theory and had talked incessantly about wanting the police to find whoever shot him. People had seemed surprised, seeing her so affected by Jason's death. Selena had to admit, if only to herself, that she'd shown only minimal affection for Jason while he was alive. Now, affection-be-damned, it was her fear of not receiving the insurance money that upset her. What if his death were declared a suicide?

"Have the police said anything new about what happened to Jason?" Owen asked when Selena returned from the kitchen. She arranged herself on the sofa, making sure that one shapely leg peeked out of the robe.

Sounding weak and helpless she said, "If they have new ideas, they haven't bothered to tell me." She sighed. "I hate this not knowing. How can I make any plans for my future when I don't know about the insurance?" Leaning toward Owen she said, frustration clear in her voice, "Suicide or murder—it makes all the difference with the insurance company." Pouting, she added, "It's not fair."

Owen nodded. "I understand. The not knowing would upset anyone in your position. I wish there were something I could do to ease your mind." Owen put his hand reassuringly on hers. "I feel somewhat responsible for you since it was my boat that disappeared."

"Your support during the days when Jason was missing and your help through the shock of the finding of his body in the bay have been my greatest comfort," she said, her voice soft. "I couldn't have survived the anxiety of the body's examination by the police, burial, and endless questions of the investigation, had you not been by my side."

Owen said, "I'm in the same situation as you. They haven't found my boat yet, so no one knows if it was stolen or went down—and by accident or on purpose." He withdrew his hand and, leaning back in his chair again, added, "I certainly sympathize with your impatience."

Selena knew that Jason had more than once urged Owen to upgrade the equipment on the *Halibut Hunter* but each time Owen refused. She knew his reluctance had angered Jason, as it reduced the number of sportsmen who would charter the boat, and therefore limited the return on the percentage he earned as his share of the income. She hadn't been happy about that decision either. The small income had been the source of many of their marital arguments. Now, Owen's attentions presented another opportunity. He appeared interested in her welfare, maybe in her personally. She hadn't considered him a possible date before. But now . . .?

She let a shade of annoyance come into her voice. "There are the kids." She frowned. "I'm not too worried about Angela. She and Kelly will get together eventually." She was aware that Jason's wretched children didn't like her—and the feeling was mutual. *How could I have been so stupid as to think that playing step-mom would be something I might enjoy? Dumb, dumb!* Selena continued, "It's Vin that's the problem. When he's not out doing 'nothing,' he's prowling around the house. He doesn't talk much. It's his silent presence that makes me uncomfortable."

Because of their watchfulness she had been very careful not to let the kids, or Jason, know about her extracurricular activities. The kids couldn't suspect her of doing drugs—could they? That Vin was sharp. If he knew anything about her drugs, he hadn't told his father. She'd often wondered if Vin suspected she used. Could he know where the drugs came from? Was he intending to spy on her to find out? Vin might not have wanted to upset Jason when he was obviously troubled about his business, but now, that constraint no longer existed. Vin might easily turn malicious. She had moved her stash out to Reynaldo's condo in the hope of hiding it from the kids. So far, Vin had said nothing.

With an artistic shudder, she took a sip of her coffee. It was cold. She rose and went to the kitchen to warm it up. When she returned to the sofa, Owen said, "I know. It's always hard to come into an established family. You took on a difficult job."

"You're right about that. I thought I could get along with those kids. Instead, they've turned into suspicious enemies. I don't know what I'm going to do." She shook her head and looked down, assuming her most distressed pose. *Vin can watch as much as he wants. I've had long practice in keeping secrets. God, what a relief it would be to get him out of the house and in RCCC, the community college. His absence would be worth whatever it cost. If I work this right, the cost can be Owen's rather than mine. All I need is to persuade Owen to pay up. Then when Angela moves in with Kelly, I will be free. It's obvious she's hooked on him. Why does the little bitch keep putting him off?*

"As I said, I've been thinking about you," Owen said, his voice gentle. "You deserve a better life than you've had here. My investments have been good recently. Perhaps I could provide the money for Vin to go to those computer classes he wants. It really isn't that expensive, and would solve one of your problems."

"Owen, you can't imagine what a relief it would be for me." Selena was delighted. It was turning out to be so easy. "It would give that boy something to do besides annoy me."

"I'd like to see you happy and living the life you ought to have. Maybe, when this is all settled, we could get together and talk about less serious subjects." He smiled. "Up to now, our conversations have dwelt mostly on problems. Perhaps we could change that." He rose and headed for the door. "We'll get together again."

Thinking, *you can count on that, buddy*, she said, "I'd like that, Owen. Thanks much."

CHAPTER TEN

All the panels were sanded; many already wearing their first coat of primer. Kira looked forward to the initial transfer of her design, which would begin tomorrow. Before that could happen, Jackie said that members of the mural committee should informally deliberate the question of the *Halibut Hunter.*

Jackie, Owen, and Kira, in one car, and Nathan, Don, Angela, and Kelly, in two others, drove to the Panting Puffin, a local gift shop and deli. After some lunch to fortify the members, would come the time for deliberation and final agreement, if that were possible.

The restaurant looked uninvitingly small from the street, but Kira soon realized that this appearance was misleading, as the space inside extended back for several rooms. In the front was a gift shop with everything from aprons, jewelry, and cards, to small items of home décor and sculpture. Behind this room was the food preparation area and order space, contained behind a glass-fronted counter, where hungry people could order sandwiches, soup, salads, or outrageous desserts. Past the counter was a small eating area with light-colored wooden tables and chairs, seating perhaps twenty guests. Large windows in the back, east-facing wall let in plenty of sunlight. Artwork, hung by local artists hoping for a sale, further brightened the room.

The mural group ordered lunches, then found a vacant table in the small dining room. A rotund man with slicked back, thinning hair was settled at a neighboring table, a bowl of soup before him. Owen introduced Kira to the man, Tony Barstow, a manager at one of the local fish processing plants and member of the Chamber of Commerce. Barstow briefly reminded Owen of the Chamber's next meeting, and asked about the progress on the mural.

By the time the food was served, the group was already deeply involved in discussing the community's response to the call for volunteers. The list of names indicated there would be an adequate turnout of painters, but there was concern that more people had not volunteered. Barstow, overhearing the talk, asked if he could slide his chair over and join the conversation. Several group members moved their chairs closer together to make space for him and his unfinished soup. Jackie whispered to Kira that Tony Barstow was one of the more conservative members of the Chamber, and known to value the past ways above more modern, unproven ones.

The subject of the *Halibut Hunter* came up quickly. "I see no reason to change the design," Jackie said. "We liked what Kira proposed. We sent her information about all the ships, including the *Halibut,* and later we unanimously approved her design. It is still a good design and I think we should stick with our decision."

Now Tony barged into the conversation, saying, "Tiedemann's body shows up on the rocks of the bay with a bullet wound— sorry, Angela, but that's the truth—and you call that no reason to remove the *Halibut Hunter* from the mural? I say that's reason enough to question what was going on out there."

Jackie drew a slow breath. "You don't know what happened. No one does. It could have been piracy for all we know—or even suicide. The police haven't come to a final decision. No one seems to have a clear idea of the possible cause. I think it unfair to make a judgment right now."

Nathan put his fork down and spoke, his usually genial expression absent. "I agree. We shouldn't try to second-guess the police. Who are we to jump to conclusions when they can't figure it out with all their scientific methods? It's only rumor that Jason was doing anything wrong." He wiped his mustache with a napkin. "There's no proof of drugs or anything else. Just his reticence in revealing the reason for, and the projected length of, his trip. Maybe he just wanted to get away for a while."

Angela, pale of face, spoke up. "My father would never do what you are hinting at, Mr. Barstow. He was a good person."

Kira detected a slight shaking in the girl's voice.

Angela continued, "Sure, he'd been quiet lately. Worried, I suppose. He had bills like everyone else. But no matter what you say, I just know he wouldn't have done anything illegal." In a small voice, she added, "I'm positive he would never consider suicide."

Barstow cast a sympathetic glance at Angela. "I understand your feelings about the talk that's going around and your wanting Jason memorialized in the painting. But consider. If you do the mural without the *Halibut Hunter,* it will help quiet all the talk. There'll no longer be anything to debate, and the dissention will probably fade away. If you leave the boat in, it's likely to ratchet up the controversy." He looked around at the others, seeming to seek their support and approval.

"If we do the mural without the *Halibut Hunter,*" Jackie said, wiping her hands on her napkin and leaning toward Tony, "everyone will be sure we thought he was smuggling. That would not be fair to Jason . . . or to Angela and Vin."

Kelly was no longer silent. "Is this debate reasonable? Someone may simply have stolen the boat and killed Jason and Randy." He frowned, adding, "It's possible he may have intended to be out for only a day. No one knows. Remember, they haven't found Randy yet. If he's still alive, he should be able to tell what really happened. Hell, he may even have been the one who shot Jason."

"Jason wasn't originally suspected of wrong doing," Nathan said, "but drugs are a problem all over Alaska. Here in Raven Creek, too. Where do they come from? I agree that no one thought Jason was doing anything questionable until he disappeared, but his death does make one wonder."

"It doesn't make me wonder," Kelly mumbled, his hands gripping the edge of the table. "Lots of drugs come hidden in trucks, or are flown in. Boats aren't the only way. Why jump to conclusions—unlikely ones at best?"

Don had been leaning his chair back against the rough textured green wall. Now, he dropped his chair down to its four legs and said, "Speaking as someone who spends a lot of time with teenagers, I see drugs becoming a problem in our schools—throughout Alaska for that matter. Youngsters I once thought would be achievers with good futures are now caught up in drugs. They have caved in to mediocrity, or tried to escape reality with marijuana, heroin, or worse. The problem isn't only in the big towns. The small native villages have the same issues. Alcohol and drugs are everywhere."

Kira wasn't surprised when Tony said, "I don't know about that. Most of the kids I see seem okay. Vin and his friends hang out at Owen's boatyard." He turned to Owen as though for confirmation. "They're all right, aren't they? I haven't noticed any problems with them, other than the changes that come with growing up."

Owen nodded his agreement.

Angela said, "Vin says he's noticed changes in a couple of the guys, maybe due to family problems, but it might be drugs. They say they can get drugs whenever they want. They don't say where or who from." She picked up her coffee cup to drink, wiped up the coffee ring on the table with her paper napkin, and again fell silent.

Tony looked at her and shrugged. "Probably just bragging on their part. It's normal at that age. Besides, this is a small town. Where would good kids like that get the stuff?"

"You'd be surprised how easy it is." Don slammed his fist on the table. "They talk to each other, you know. They can always find some if they want to." He shook his head in obvious frustration. "If I had my way I would strangle the people who supply the drugs. They ruin the lives of so many. Many teens here have few outside activities to keep them occupied, no special interests. They're the ones in danger. Ask any drug counselor—which we don't have here in town, but could certainly use."

Tony Barstow spoke again. "We're getting off the subject. The question is the *Halibut Hunter*. I still think including the boat is an insult to our town and indicates our approval of dishonesty and drug running." His face had reddened during the discussion. "What kind of reputation will our town have if we continue the way you all seem to want?"

"Calm down and consider, Tony," Nathan said. "You can't have it both ways. You say there are no drugs in town, then immediately accuse Jason of smuggling some in. Which is it?"

Don said, "We don't have to decide immediately. I suggest we leave the *Halibut Hunter* in for now. If problems or damning facts arise in the future, the boat can be painted out." He looked around the group. "I was originally in favor of not including it because of gossip. Now I'm beginning to agree with Jackie. We can wait a little longer, keep an open mind about what to do, and see what happens."

Kira, having been silent throughout the discussion, finally said, "I've hesitated to speak until now. This is your town, and I'm only a visitor. But I believe I provided a good design for the mural. I would like to see us continue as planned. Does anyone really think that all the other boats being commemorated were one hundred percent pure and free of all questionable cargo? I don't. The reading I did in preparation for my design indicated that lots of funny things have gone on over the years. I'd like to see you carry on without making changes. Either way there will be talk, but this way we will not be making a judgment. I've heard no facts to justify changing the mural, just suspicion and rumor." She looked at the people gathered around the table and thought they seemed to be good people who sincerely cared for their town and wanted to do the right thing in this situation—if they could only figure out what the right thing was.

After a little more discussion, they agreed they could put off the decision since they didn't know anything for sure. They finished their lunches and returned to the terminal.

CHAPTER ELEVEN

Tuesday

At breakfast, as Jackie put the last of the serving dishes on the table, she said, "Warren, there must be something you can do, people you could talk to. The rumors about Jason and smuggling are making the volunteers uncomfortable."

Kira knew Jackie had been increasingly worried about the dissention engendered by having the *Halibut Hunter* in the painting. She thought Jackie was more worried than the situation warranted, but hesitated to say anything. As an outsider, Kira felt unable to clearly appreciate all the undercurrents in the town.

"Me? What can I do?" Warren sounded bewildered as he slid his omelet onto his plate. "I set up websites. I'm not an investigator or a miracle worker. Do you want me to stop the rumors about Jason, or discover who's doing the smuggling? Or perhaps you think I'm Sherlock Holmes and can discover who is selling the stuff?"

"Oh, I don't know." Jackie's hands gestured her confusion. "It's just that there is so much talk. Someone should do something."

"I agree," Warren said, and swallowed a forkful of eggs, "but what you are asking me to do is a job for the police. I don't begin to have the information or investigative tools they have and they would not thank me for sticking my nose into their business."

"As far as I can see they don't seem to be doing anything about the problem," Jackie said. She got up and walked to the window. Turning back to the table she continued, "Why aren't they doing more? Don't they care?"

"I'm sure they are working on it," Kira said, adding, "What else do you think they should be doing?"

"I don't know," Jackie said. "There is so much money involved—and the police are only human. Could one or more of them be helping the smugglers? You know, misdirecting the investigation or something?"

Pausing to sip his coffee, Warren said, "I suppose it's possible. You hear of such things. But do you really think it's likely? This is a small town. Wouldn't people know?"

"Nobody seems to care enough to check on it. The newspaper might have a reporter looking into it, but would they really want to go up against the police department? I doubt it."

"I understand your concern, but what can I do to help?" Warren pushed his plate back. "I've heard the same rumors about drugs in town. I suppose everyone has, or at least those who are willing to listen."

"You should hear Don talking about the problem," Jackie said. "The idea of students caught up in the drug scene infuriates him. If he found a pusher, I think he would hang him from the nearest tree and feel totally justified in doing it." Her hands clenched. "And I wouldn't blame him."

"He cares a lot for his students," Kira said, as she refilled her glass of orange juice. "You can tell by the way he talks about them. From what Nathan has told me, he's an outstanding teacher, one who really wants to see the kids succeed."

"The painting seems to repeatedly bring the subject of smuggling to everyone's attention," Jackie said.

"Are you sure that my meddling won't call even more attention to it?" Warren asked. "Come on back and finish your breakfast," he invited Jackie. "No need to go hungry over this. Lots of people don't believe illegal substances are a problem, and they sure don't want to hear about it. They might have to act and they don't want to do that either."

Kira thought she understood why Warren hesitated to get drawn in to any investigation. He probably wanted to see the problem resolved, but didn't think he was the one to attempt doing it, believing it was more than a one-person job. Better to leave it to the law.

Returning to her chair, Jackie began to eat, even as she continued making plans for Warren. "I've been trying to think of people who might know something—I mean, outside of students. Maybe trucking company drivers or cruise ship crewmembers would have some ideas, but they'd be hard to find, and then they probably wouldn't admit to knowing anything." She stopped to take a breath. "There is the Coast Guard. Maybe they . . ."

"Okay, okay," Warren said, apparently realizing he would have to do something to ease Jackie's distress. "Slow down. I'll try to talk with some of the kids at the school when I go there tomorrow afternoon to help the computer club. They know me and might tell me something they wouldn't tell the police. It won't hurt to ask, but knowing how secretive they can be about the actions of their friends, I don't think I'll learn anything."

Jackie was obviously relieved at Warren's capitulation. "Oh, Warren, thank you." She got up from her chair to walk over and kiss him on the top of his head. "Anything you learn will help." Then she added, "Don't forget, the principal, or teachers could have ideas. They might hesitate to get directly involved with talking to officials, but they may talk to you."

"If I have a chance, I'll talk to them, too," Warren said with a sigh.

CHAPTER TWELVE

The breeze off Harpoon Bay sent the wind gauges spinning atop the masts of the small boats in the harbor. Long gray clouds straggled over the surrounding mountains, tearing themselves apart on the peaks, only to regroup in the valleys. Close to shore, eagles searched for fish. Seagulls rested along streambeds or squabbled on black rock piles in the gravel company yard. Ravens of the town scoured trash bins in search of tasty tidbits, while others circled the coal transport yard or perched near the coal conveyer just west of the cruise line terminal.

Every other week, ships from Korea arrived at the Northwestern Coal Company's loading dock to pick up their cargo. Between their visits, long heavily-laden trains from the interior came to replace the coal taken away in the previous shipment. In summer, cruise ships tied up nearby. An area to the west of the terminal was busy with trucks loading the small cargo ships that serviced the many villages along the Alaska coast. Heavy bags of sand, concrete, canned goods, and other assorted necessities were piled on their decks. The pace of work was moderate throughout the entire complex. Jobs were done without fuss or hurry.

It was the black bear that drew people's attention. He was first noticed as he sniffed the air and prowled in the weeds next to the chain link fence surrounding the coal yard. Many bears lived in the hills around Raven Creek. Some came into town occasionally. But there was nothing to eat where this one roamed, no trashcans or dumpsters. He hadn't climbed the fence—yet—but bears were climbers, and it could happen. If he did get inside the coal yard, it would be difficult to chase him away. A cornered and confused bear could be dangerous.

Hikers in the surrounding forest were instructed to keep a sharp watch for the animals, not walk alone, and to make noise or talk to each other. Stores sold "bear bells" for visitors to wear, so the bears would hear them and move away. The locals joked that a better name for the bells would be "dinner bells." They helped the bears more easily find a tasty tourist.

The coal yard next to the terminal was longer than a football field, enclosed on three sides by eight-foot chain-link fencing. A loading dock and the waters of Harpoon Bay completed the fourth side. An enclosed conveyer belt for loading coal into ships ran along one side of the area. Although it had occasional gaps for inspection, and funnel-shaped openings for loading by truck, the only way to get across the mechanism was by using the few widely spaced ladders that had been built over its curved metal cowling.

The police were first to arrive on the scene after receiving 911 calls about the wandering bear. They watched the animal for a few minutes, hoping it would leave when confronted by the sirens of their squad cars. They knew better than to park too close. Bear claws could ruin a paint job in short order. When it became obvious the animal was not intimidated by their presence, the officers decided on a spray of bear repellent safely administered from inside the coal yard fence.

Devlin Fossinger, the coal yard manager, was called to unlock the side gate to allow Officer Winston to enter the area. Devlin seemed happy to let the man in and relieved not to be required to accompany the officer along the fence.

For Officer Winston, the walk to where the animal was scratching at the base of the fence and growling softly, seemed endless. Hemmed in by the conveyer, now unused and resting quietly only fifteen feet behind him and blocking retreat in that direction, Winston was uncomfortably aware that he would be hard put to escape should the bear suddenly decide to charge over the wire barrier.

Speaking in his most commanding voice, he ordered, "Git! Scram! Move your butt!" The bear stopped pacing for a moment and gave the officer a cold lingering look. Winston wondered if he was being considered as a possible snack.

"Go on. Git!" he said again, louder this time. The bear lowered its head, turned away slightly, and glanced back at him out of the corners of its eyes. With that, Winston raised the can of repellent and gave *Ursus Americanus* a sample spray. Fortunately, it was just a sample. He had forgotten to check the wind direction. Too late he realized it was blowing from the north, right into his face.

The bear sneezed, slapped the fence angrily several times with its paws, smacked its lips, and huffed. Officer Winston was the one who coughed, covered his eyes, and abruptly left the area. The bear calmly watched him stumble away. Then, with another huff, got on with his digging.

During this interlude, the fire department's truck had arrived. The men had watched the confrontation and its result and decided their assistance was needed. After consulting with a still partially-blinded Winston and his partner, they initiated a united, two pronged, ursine removal attack.

In a short time, sirens, complements of the police cruiser, and a water shower, gratis from the fire department, were deployed. It was a fine show of public servants working together for the good of the community. Better yet, there was a positive outcome in that the bear, wet and loudly complaining but uninjured, was finally chased back into the woods. Acknowledging the congratulations of onlookers and late-arriving local press and complimenting each other on the success of their teamwork, the warriors for the community turned off their sirens, packed their fire hoses, and triumphantly drove away.

*   *   *

Two hours later, Devlin Fossinger looked out the south window of his office. The number and unusual behavior of ravens and seagulls gathered around the coal conveyer aroused his curiosity. Following the bear excitement of the morning, he was alert to anything out of the ordinary. Telling himself he could use some exercise, he descended from the second floor of the coal company's small headquarters building and walked across the dark-gray gravel of the yard toward where the peculiar activity of the birds was centered. He saw nothing of interest in the area where they flocked, nor anything out of order about the equipment. He moved closer to check out the stationary conveyer belt, wiggled the metal sheets covering some sections to be sure they were securely attached, pulled on the belt to test the tension, and looked inside to see that it was clear. What he found sent him running back to his office to call the police. Within five minutes of his call, two official vans arrived to be met by Devlin who, for the second time that day, unlocked the gates to let the police in.

Parking in front of the main building, Officer Winston and a bulky man with crew-cut hair and wearing everyday dress, got out. The latter introduced himself as Detective Savarous. Two other men from the second vehicle joined him. Savarous identified them as a technician and police photographer.

"I was in the office when your call came in," Savarous said. "So thought I would come to see what you found. I prefer to be in at the beginning whenever possible."

Fossinger's voice shook. "It was horrible—I mean—a body. And all that blood! I didn't stay to look at it. I just got to the phone as fast as I could." He stopped to catch his breath. "It's out there, where all the birds are." He pointed across the yard. "I wondered what was attracting them. I never guessed . . ." His voice trailed off . . .

"Officer Winston and I will check out the area," Savarous said, "and talk with you later in your office." The men dispersed, Fossinger unsteadily to his office, Winston and Savarous to the conveyer, the others to their vehicles to collect the equipment they would need.

CHAPTER THIRTEEN

The bear incident in the morning distracted everyone, especially Kira, from work on the mural. She'd never seen a wild bear and was fascinated to learn what was done to make it leave without hurting it. She stayed outside watching until the last fire truck turned toward town. For the other mural volunteers, bears in town were an old story, so they returned to work after a short look at the scene.

In the afternoon the mural activity moved into a new phase. With two coats of primer on most of the panels, it was time to set up the projector and transfer the original artwork onto them. This would take at least two full days. Susan Goreman, a quiet, thirty-something woman with dark curly hair, whom Kira was meeting for the first time, would operate the projector. She repeatedly vowed to all who would listen that next year they would use a computer to do this part of the job.

She planned to project individual sections of the painting on the large boards placed vertically against the wall so the enlarged and transferred image would be as free of distortion as possible. Using marking pens, three or four volunteers would then trace around the projected image shapes. After each board received its portion of the design and the individual spaces were numbered to indicate the appropriate color to be applied, it would be removed and another put in its place.

Jackie told Kira she was happy to see her entire work crew waiting when they returned to the terminal after lunch. With Don, Nathan, Owen, Kelly and Angela, plus Susan and two others helping, the work should progress rapidly.

Kira and Jackie stood back to observe the volunteers stooping and stretching to copy the projected lines onto the boards. "People sure look strange with the lines sliding over their bodies as they move around," Kira said. "It's disconcerting. After watching for a while, they seem to become part of the surface in front of them. I have to look away to get back to reality."

"It's difficult to keep your body out of the way of the design," Jackie said. "You get involved in tracing and suddenly the line disappears into your own shadow as you lean forward with your marker."

The drawing transfer went smoothly. By late afternoon eleven panels, ready for painting, were laid out on the tables. If they could keep up the pace, all twenty-eight boards would have their design in place by Thursday.

When the real painting began on Friday, Jackie told Kira, many more people would come to help. However, much preparation was needed before the final painting could begin, and Kira was constantly aware that something unforeseen could happen to throw the entire project off schedule.

She looked up in surprise as Nathan burst into the cruise terminal from a trip to the store for additional marking pens and blurted out, "You'll never guess what happened," He tossed the sack of new pens he had bought onto the projector table. "They've found a body next door in the coal yard!"

People immediately surrounded him, asking questions faster that he could answer them.

"A body!"

"Who was it?" someone shouted.

"When did they find it?"

Nathan held up his hand for quiet and explained that he'd stopped to listen to some of the onlookers' conversations on his way back from the store. "I think they discovered it shortly after I left here. There was nothing unusual over there when I drove off. I suppose, with the terminal doors closed, you folks couldn't see what was going on outside."

As he continued talking, Kira joined the mural volunteers rushing to shrug into their jackets to go outside and see for themselves. This event was far more interesting than a bear sighting.

As they all hurried out the front doors, Kira asked, "Was it an accident? Did one of the workers fall? It's been quiet over there this week, except for the bear incident this morning."

Nathan raised his voice. "The body was on the conveyer belt, about sixty feet behind the main office, but back under the metal cowling so it wouldn't be noticed easily." His listeners peered across the parking lot toward the coal yard where several officers were standing in quiet conversation. Others worked around the conveyer. Still more were slowly searching both sides of the fence. An ambulance was just driving away from the main building.

"On the conveyer belt? Don said. "How odd. I didn't know it was running. Did a worker get caught in the machinery?"

"It wasn't running and it wasn't an accident," Nathan replied. "I'll bet the poor guy was murdered." Exclamations of alarm came from his listeners.

"Why do you say that? Could you see anything when you drove by?" someone asked.

"Well, if the conveyer wasn't working, what else but murder would explain the body?" Nathan replied.

"Who found him?" Jackie asked.

"It seems Fossinger was the lucky one, although that's probably not the word I should use. I saw him looking out the office window when I was there. He looked pale, shocked. I can just picture his distress when he found the body. He likes things neat and organized. Train arrivals and shipping schedules please him. Dead bodies wouldn't."

"What made him go out there?" Kira asked, arms hugging her ribs. The thought of finding a body in such an unlikely place chilled her.

"That's what's strange, Kira. From what people were saying when I stopped over there, Fossinger looked out his window and noticed birds flapping around one of the openings in the belt cover. After this morning's bear confrontation, he was jumpy. He couldn't figure out why so many birds would be attracted to such an unlikely place. So, on a break, he went to look."

"Does anyone know who it is?" Don asked.

"The word is it's Reynaldo—the man who works for Owen Martin," Nathan answered. "Nobody I talked with saw the body clearly when it was removed from the belt, but that's what they're saying."

At this, Angela and Kelly moved away from the group. The two huddled wordlessly together, their eyes still fixed on the activity in the coal yard.

Her hands stuffed into her pockets, Jackie asked, "Who would want to kill him, and why? He's never been in trouble or even slightly controversial, or if he was, I never heard."

"The opposite, in fact," Nathan added, smirking. "Colorless and boring."

"Why would his body be there? He'd have no reason to be in the coal yard," Jackie continued. "He usually worked with Owen. Bookkeeper, wasn't he?"

"That's right." He looked around. Angela and Kelly had moved away from the group. Nathan continued in a softer voice, "Since those two aren't near, I can repeat what some of the people over by the fence are starting to say." He lowered his voice to a whisper. "The fact is, that Reynaldo has been seen around town with Selena, especially lately. The police are sure to know that and will probably question her and the kids. All the controversy over their father's death—and now this. It's going to be tough on them."

Susan Goreman, who until then had been silent, said, "It will be hard on Owen, too. Those two men have worked together a long time, usually at Owen's office in town, but sometimes out at the boatyard. How strange that his bookkeeper should be killed. This will be a sad time for him. Do you think he will be willing to come back and help at the paint table?"

Jackie looked around the group. "Now that you mention it, where is Owen? I saw him talking on his cell phone a while ago. Maybe the police called him to come in. If it's Reynaldo who was killed, the police will definitely want to talk to Owen, maybe have him officially identify the body."

Fifteen minutes later most of the volunteers still sat on the concrete planters in front of the terminal, watching the continuing activity at the coal yard. The frost-killed flowers Kira had previously noticed on her initial arrival at the terminal on Saturday remained crumpled and brown in the dirt. They seemed a fitting commentary on the present situation.

"I don't understand the conveyer belt thing," Kira said. "The location is bizarre. Did the killer think a body would never be found there—or maybe he thought Reynaldo's body would go to Korea with the next coal shipment."

"Now, that's a wild idea." Nathan brightened. "I wonder if it would have worked?" He appeared to find the situation amusing.

Don craned his neck to see the end of the conveyer. "I doubt it. The loading tube that feeds the coal into the ships looks too small to let a body through."

Jackie sighed. "What a day! A bear in the morning, and a murder in the afternoon."

Nathan exclaimed, "Say, do you think the bear knew Reynaldo's body was inside the fenced area? I mean, could the animal have smelled him or something? I wonder how long his body was there or if anyone knows when he died?"

"I hadn't considered that," Don replied, looking toward the area of the fence where the bear had been. "The animal was near where the police are searching. He quite possibly could have picked up the scent. Bears are famous for having an incredible sense of smell. Now that I think about it, the birds may also have been aware of the odor. Gulls are scavengers. As to your other question, I would guess it's too early to know when he died."

Nathan looked over to the weed-covered area where they'd seen the bear that morning. Officers were still carefully going over the ground. He said, "Good luck to the police. After all the people trampling around there today, plus the water from the fire hose, I doubt there will be much left to find. The water probably washed away any footprints or other clues."

"I hope not all of them," Jackie said. "I don't know about you, but I've had enough excitement and mysterious happenings this summer. A missing deckhand, a body in the bay—reason for death still undetermined—and now Reynaldo. Too much has happened and too much remains unknown." She turned and walked back into the quiet terminal, followed by several others in the group. Kira remained outside.

Angela and Kelly still stood apart. They, too, were watching the police. Kira saw Kelly's arm wrap protectively around Angela. If it really was Reynaldo who had been found, as people were saying, Kira was sure there would be additional questions for them from the police, and more controversy in the town about the Tiedemann family. And now, because of Selena carrying on with Reynaldo, their peace would again be shattered. Would the nightmare of this summer never end?

Earlier that morning Angela had mentioned to Kira that she and Vin had recently noticed a change in Selena's manner. She was more distant and quiet, yet with an undertone of excitement. They thought it a result of her reactivated social life and her awareness of their disapproval of it. Angela said that most of the time they didn't know where Selena was going when she left the house—she wouldn't tell them . . . and they didn't care. Her absence was their gain.

Now, Kira was near enough to hear Angela say, "Wouldn't you know? Selena has done it again!" Her voice carried a mixture of anger and disgust. "Has she no sense at all? Her seeing that man so often, especially recently and in public, and then being out all last night. Won't that just look great during an investigation?" Angela seemed to almost choke on her anger. "This murder will upset everything. Selena had better have a darn good excuse for not coming home."

CHAPTER FOURTEEN

Shortly after the corpse was removed from the coal yard and sent to the medical examiner, clouds lowered and the rain began. The storm introduced itself with gusts of wind chilled from the mountains, then intensified into a soaking downpour. Owen Martin reluctantly made his way through the blustery storm to the morgue. Savarous, an acquaintance of Owen's since his childhood, had called him to come and identify the body. Once inside and gazing at the remains of Reynaldo, Owen felt the blood drain from his face. He stared at the wound where Reynaldo's throat had been cut. In the past he had spent many hours hooking, gaffing, and cleaning fish, as well as hanging and gutting the larger animals he'd hunted in the forest around the state. Still, in spite of his previous experience with blood and death, seeing Reynaldo's long-dead body was unsettling.

The cold, gusty wind, laced with rain, sought violent entry through the windows of the office where Owen and the police went to talk after viewing Reynaldo's body. The drops, like tiny wet fists, were hurled against the panes and instantly shattered, only to reconstitute into a multitude of runnels fleeing across the glass. Owen felt the weather's chill settle deep in his bones, the grayness implanting itself in his spirit. Death was so quiet and final. Though his body remained, the reality of Reynaldo was gone beyond recall, his presence in Owen's office ended, his voice, discussing an obscure financial twist, now forever silenced.

Owen had difficulty concentrating on the questions the police asked. Apparently, aware of his distraction, they released him with notice that they would continue the conversation at a later time.

*   *   *

At home, after fixing a simple evening meal, Owen sat in his softly lighted study recalling the past years of his and Reynaldo's association. His glass of bourbon was empty. The newspaper in his hands was only a thin wall against memories.

When the doorbell rang, he reluctantly put down the paper, slowly got up from his favorite chair, and made his way through the darkened living room to the front hall. The shadowy figures of two men showed through the frosted glass in the door. *The police. Again?*

Opening the door, Owen was confronted by Detective Savarous and Officer Winston. They'd told him they would be leading the subsequent investigation, since they'd been the first officers notified when the body was found,

Cold wind followed them into the hall, swirling around their damp shoulders. "Good evening, Owen," Detective Savarous said. "Now that you've had time to recover from your initial distress, we have some more questions we'd like to ask."

Owen wondered what would happen if he called Savarous by his given name. He imagined Savarous would probably see it as a sign of disrespect. He invited them to follow him into his study. "I'm having a drink. It's been a sad day for me. Can I offer you something or is it against regulations?" As he spoke, he picked up his empty glass from the table and walked to the well-stocked bar at the far end of the room. Its distressed copper top and mahogany panels gleamed warmly in the low light of the room. Owen always felt comfortable in this space, the quiet ambiance soothing after a stressful day at the office or boatyard. He knew he was going to need that calmness in the coming minutes. Savarous refused drinks for both of them.

Owen refilled his glass and turned back to the visitors. "Please, make yourselves comfortable." He indicated several chairs scattered invitingly about the room. "Have you learned any more since this afternoon?"

Winston appeared mild mannered, with slightly graying hair, a thin, lined face, and a body that showed the effect of years of physical training and a reasonable diet. He settled into an armchair next to a small table topped with a heavily shaded lamp. Savarous, more bulky than Winston—almost flabby—with the air of an arrogant, self-righteous zealot, chose a more upright seat. "There's not much we can tell you at this time," the detective announced sonorously. "The investigation's just getting started. We've come to see if you've had any new thoughts about what happened to Mr. Lovato."

Owen slowly sipped his drink. "This entire situation seems so unlikely." His brow furrowed in puzzlement. "I can't imagine who or why anyone would want to do such a horrible thing to him." His voice trembled as he spoke.

"How well did you know Mr. Lovato? Specifically, who were his friends?" Savarous asked. "What kind of person was he? Well liked? A loner?"

This detective wasted no time on preliminaries.

Owen's voice softened in reminiscence as he said, "Reynaldo worked for me for approximately five years. We didn't socialize after hours if that's what you mean. Ours was strictly a business relationship. He was skilled at his job and easy to work with. As to his friends, I have no idea."

"What do you know about his finances? Was he in debt?" Shadows cast by the light from a corner lamp accentuated the darkness under Savarous's eyebrows.

"I doubt it. I paid him a good wage, and he never appeared to be short of cash." Owen added, "He had a nice condo and a fairly new car. I would say he was doing very well."

Apparently looking for any angle that would help him pry open a door into Reynaldo's life, Savarous asked, "Possibly too well?"

Owen thought of Reynaldo's two-bedroom condo, with its wide deck offering a splendid view of the bay. It had an upscale address that required a healthy income.

During the questioning, Officer Winston remained quietly seated in his chair. It might have been empty, for all the impact he made on the discussion. He had a notebook, into which he occasionally scribbled. His expression remained bland.

"I hardly know what else to say." Owen leaned forward. "Are you hinting he might have been involved in something illegal? As to that, I can't give you an answer. As far as I could see, he wasn't hurting for money. He didn't live flamboyantly, although that doesn't prove anything." *The police have probably been to Reynaldo's house already, so why is Savarous really asking all these questions?*

"But you must have known something about his life," Savarous persisted. "You saw him almost every day."

Sipping his drink, Owen said, "I can't give you any facts about his life outside of business hours. I run a business, and Reynaldo worked for me. He was just an employee, for God's sake. Other times we mostly went our own ways. I explained that to you at your office today."

Again Savarous pressed. "Did he have a social life? Was he interested in anyone in particular? We know he wasn't married. Did he have a girlfriend?"

Owen was beginning to resent the detective's pushy attitude. "I recently heard he was seeing Selena Tiedemann. We didn't talk about it, so I don't know if it's true, or if the relationship was serious."

"You mean the widow of the guy who was found in the bay a few months ago?"

"That's the one."

"You owned the boat Tiedemann skippered, the *Halibut Hunter*, didn't you? I would imagine you know his wife pretty well. What is she like?"

Owen looked at Savarous, while considering an answer. Suddenly, the detective had changed the subject from Reynaldo, to Jason and Selena. Owen felt a sudden need to adjust his position in his chair, but realized it would make him appear uncomfortable with the questioning. "Strangely, I don't think she was very upset about her husband's death," he said. "I'd heard she was looking around for another man even before Jason's accident."

Savarous pounced on that idea. "Was her husband aware of her activities?"

"I have no idea." It was difficult to curb his impatience. Owen wondered whom Savarous was trying to impress. "Jason handled my boat for me," he said. "He didn't confide in me about his family life."

After a pause the detective continued. "Do you know how Selena Tiedemann's children feel about her possible interest in Mr. Lovato? For instance, do they like him?"

"Angela and Vin?" Owen looked at Winston for a moment, then back to Savarous. "They are her stepchildren, her husband's children, not hers. I don't think they get along well—the stepmother thing, I suppose. I helped with the funeral arrangements after Jason was found, and I gave a little business advice to Selena. Other than that, I don't know much. As to your question, I imagine if she had warmed up to Reynaldo, the kids would automatically dislike him." *I don't know what game you're trying to play with me, Savarous, but you are wasting my time—and yours. I'm not impressed.*

Savarous, still rigidly upright on his chair, seemed to want more information. "What can you tell me about the children?"

Oh, for God's sake. Enough of this. Owen adjusted his position in the chair. *To hell with what they think.* "The daughter's a sweet kid, very upset over her father's death. She has a boyfriend, Kelly Singleton. He works at the gravel company and wants to marry her. They've gone together for more than two years. I believe they were on the point of planning their marriage when her father disappeared. Now, I understand, she'll have nothing to do with the marriage idea until she knows the truth about what happened to her dad. There may be other reasons for her hesitation. I don't know." He thought of Angela's quiet demeanor and closed face.

In the time before her father's death, she had been an outgoing young woman.

"And the boy Vin?"

"He's a different story." Owen took another swallow of his drink and re-crossed his legs. He wanted to cooperate in this farce, but not too much. "He had issues with his father over finances. Vin wants to attend the local technical school. His father wouldn't pay for him to go. I heard there were bad feelings between them over that issue."

"Is he a troublemaker?" Savarous leaned forward, sounding as though he hoped the boy was.

"Oh, no." Owen was emphatic. "Vin is one of a group of kids who have hung around my boatyard for years. For the most part, they are just normal, energetic, basically good kids. Naturally, people change as they get older." He thought a bit. "I've occasionally wondered if a couple of them might be getting involved with drugs. I hope not. It's a terrible habit. I regret to say that the stuff is available in town, even if the parents won't admit it. But I guess you already know that, don't you?"

The detective looked sharply at him, then nodded.

"I doubt Vin is a user." Owen swirled his drink slowly. Then suggested, "You should probably ask Vin about his friends. He would know more than I do." He glanced at Winston, his pen still busy taking notes. Owen suspected he was attentive to every word spoken. His job seemed to be as a watcher, to provide another viewpoint for Savarous. He was the "thinker," Savarous the "bull dog."

"Let's discuss what you were doing Monday evening," Savarous moved on. "We have to ask everyone that question."

Now he's back on the murder again. Owen closed his eyes momentarily to consider. "To the best of my memory I was going through paperwork at my office in town until late—ten or eleven, as I recall. I had spent the day working with the mural group at the ship terminal, so night was the only time I had to catch up with the mail and other business."

"Was Mr. Lovato helping you that evening?"

"No. Of course not. He had gone home by the time I arrived, or at least I thought he had."

"You have a truck. Were you driving it that night?" Savarous appeared to be watching for a sign of surprise, or perhaps, fear.

Owen looked at him thoughtfully. "Yes." Then, wondering where his question was leading, inquired, "Why do you ask?"

"What would you say if I told you there were truck tire marks in the dirt outside the coal yard fence?" He looked sharply at Owen.

After a momentary pause, Owen answered, "After all the water the fire department sprayed on the bear this morning I'd say I'm surprised you found any tracks at all. If there were some, they won't be from my truck, unless it was borrowed and returned without my knowledge. Or, I suppose, if they are from my truck, which I doubt, they might be left over from the times I've driven to the terminal." *Do you think I'm fool enough to go along with this ploy of yours? Tracks, my ass.*

"Does that seem likely or even possible?"

"That I'd made the tracks some other time when I went to the terminal, or that my truck was borrowed that night? Either might be possible. Unlikely, but possible. As I said, I was at my office for several hours that evening," He set his drink down and leaned back. "The truck could have been taken by anyone, I suppose. It's always parked behind my building. I seldom bother to take the keys out."

Seeming to have decided to downplay the tire print aspect of the questioning, Savarous said, "With all the activity over there, police cars, fire trucks, and people moving around, the tracks we found may have no connection with the murder, but we'll be checking to see if we can identify the vehicle. We think it's possible the body was transported in the back of a pickup, then lifted over the fence, and carried to the conveyer belt. We need to look at the trucks of all people even remotely concerned in this business."

Owen glanced at Winston to see if his face showed any reaction to what was occurring. His face gave nothing away. *Is he alive?* Owen wondered. He looked back to Savarous and said, "I've driven to the terminal, next to the coal yard, every day this week. I'm sure my tire marks will be found somewhere around the area." After a pause he added, "Let me remind you I'm not the only one working there that has a truck. Kelly Singleton, Don Lansing, and many others also have pickups. This town is full of them."

The detective raised a hand reassuringly. "Well, I wouldn't worry if I were you. As I said, the tracks were indistinct. This may turn out to be a dead end."

This entire question and answer thing was a sham, Owen thought. Savarous simply wanted to root around in his mind a bit, unsettle him with his apparent mistrust. He wasn't asking him anything that couldn't be found out another way.

Savarous abruptly rose. Winston put his notebook in his pocket and joined him. "We will be in touch again if we have any more questions," Savarous said. "You are planning to stay in town the rest of the week, aren't you?"

Wondering if that was a question or an order from the "bull dog," Owen said, "I will be working at the terminal, at least until Sunday. The work on the mural has just begun, and I promised to help." He was maintaining his dignity with difficulty, as his nerves had taken a beating from this interview. He added, "I will be available whenever you need me." Savarous nodded and the three moved toward the front door. As the visitors were leaving, Owen said, "I hope you find the person who did this atrocity. I can't imagine who could have hated him that much."

"Oh, we'll get the killer all right." Savarous's broad chin came up, and he straightened his shoulders. "It will take some work, but we'll get him."

But will you dare arrest him? Owen wondered.

CHAPTER FIFTEEN

Wednesday

By the time she and Jackie arrived at the terminal, Kira was delighted to see that the skies had partially cleared after the storm of the previous day. For a few minutes she watched the shadows of broken clouds race up and down the rocky sides of the mountains surrounding Otter Bay. She hoped the sunlight would lift the spirits of the volunteers gathered in the darkened building for the day's work.

Kira was full of energy and ready to forge ahead with tracing the mural design. She was pleased to see the growing number of prepared panels at rest on the tables and ready for the volunteers who, paintbrushes in hand, would be bending over them during the weekend.

The volunteers from Tuesday—Susan, Don, Nathan, Kelly, and Angela—were present and had begun working. Kira would not have been surprised if Owen were absent, but he, too, had come to work. The expression on his face appeared more solemn than on previous days, but he seemed determined to continue with his obligations, maintain a semblance of normalcy, and not let his distress distract him from his commitment to the project. She admired his self-control, noting that he was not the dramatic type who paraded his emotions for all to see.

The work of tracing the lines from the master drawing went well—until an interruption caused by the arrival of the police. Kira saw Owen's head jerk up. When she'd first arrived he'd told her a little about the police visit to his home. Upon seeing Detective Savarous and Officer Winston, whom she immediately recognized from the previous day in the coal yard, she wondered if they were there to ask him more questions.

Jackie walked over to the officers, who hesitated by the front doors of the terminal. As they talked, the work on the mural sputtered to a stop. Curiosity held most of the workers motionless.

Following a short conversation, Jackie returned to the group. "They want to talk with you, Angela," she said gently. Angela turned quickly to Kelly, a frightened look on her face. He separated himself from the group he had been helping to accompany Angela as she walked toward the waiting men.

*   *   *

"Are you Miss Angela Tiedemann?" the larger man asked gruffly.

"Yes," she responded quietly. That he was not in a uniform confused her. His curt voice and bulky physique made her uncomfortable.

"This is Officer Winston, and I am Detective Savarous," he announced in a self-important voice. "We are investigating the death of Reynaldo Lovato and want to ask you a few questions."

She nodded. "This is Kelly Singleton . . . a special friend of mine." She gripped Kelly's hand tightly as she introduced him.

Savarous said, "I'm glad you're here, Mr. Singleton. We want to talk with you, too, but right now, it's Miss Tiedemann we need. Stay around until we're finished questioning her. Then we will call you."

Kelly and Angela looked at each other, then she reluctantly let go of his hand. "I can't imagine this will take long," she told Kelly, adding, "After you're finished with their questions, we can go to lunch." She gave him a weak smile. Turning to address Detective Savarous, she asked, "Where do you want to talk?"

Seating in the mural work area was limited and the other volunteers would probably easily overhear what they said. Officer Winston pointed toward the far side of the terminal, to where the children's play section during the music festival would be. Once there, he dragged three folding chairs away from the wall, their legs scraping loudly on the concrete floor, and arranged them in a small circle.

As they sat, the chill of apprehension Angela felt wasn't just from the cold metal of the seat. Ever since learning the body found was that of Reynaldo, she'd feared she would be drawn into the investigation. Selena's connection to the man had made it almost inevitable.

After the three were seated, Savarous said, "We're sorry to take you away from your work, but we need to learn all you can tell us about Mr. Lovato. We are also looking for your mother."

Angela looked intently at him, but chose to remain silent. These were statements, not questions.

He continued, "We understand your mother was a friend of Mr. Lovato, as well as Mr. Owen Martin. We wanted to talk to her this morning. She wasn't home. Do you know where she is?"

His assumption about her relationship to Selena angered her. "She's not my mother," Angela said forcefully. Her dislike of Selena made her want to distance herself from any genetic relationship. "My father married her only a couple of years ago."

Savarous appeared unaware of the annoyance in her voice. "Do you know where she is, or how we can get in touch with her?" he asked again.

Angela glanced toward Winston, seated to the right of Savarous with his notebook and pen ready in his lap. Knowing that anything she said could be written in that book made her uncomfortable. It might have been worse, she reflected. What if he were using a tape recorder?

"I can't help you," Angela finally said. After a long pause during which the detective stared at her, she reluctantly added, "She didn't come home last night—but that's not unusual. Selena doesn't tell us her plans." After another silence, she said, "Vin, my brother, thinks she may have gone shopping in Anchorage . . . but that's just a guess."

Angela saw Savarous raise a questioning eyebrow at Winston. She'd hoped they would accept this as a possible explanation but feared her tone of voice betrayed her doubts.

The detective said, "We'd like to talk to her when she returns. Do you expect her to come home tonight?"

She shrugged and shook her head, not caring where Selena had gone or when she'd return. "I don't know. She's never been gone this long before, at least not since Dad died." She readjusted herself in her chair but found no comfort. "When he was very busy during fishing season, she would sometimes disappear for a day or two. I don't know if even Dad knew where she went. If he did, he never told us, and we didn't ask."

She and Vin hadn't wanted to worry or embarrass their father by bringing up the problems he and Selena were having. They had been unhappy observers of the slow dissolution of a marriage their father had hoped would unite them and provide a renewed sense of family. It had been a sad process to watch.

Savarous and Winston mumbled together as Winston thumbed through his notes. Angela thought again about her and Vin's relationship with their father. He'd always seemed to find it difficult to understand his children. It had been their mother who supplied the warmth in their lives. Although the kids knew he wanted to be a good provider and worked hard for what money he made, it never seemed easy for him to connect with them on an emotional level. He relied on rules and determination to organize his thinking. He could not accept human frailty in himself and he set the same standards for those around him. She knew he tried to be a loving father but didn't know how, and only came across as distant and gruff.

Savarous interrupted her thoughts. "You don't get along with Selena?" He seemed to be trying to put some gentleness in his voice, but his body language said he was ready to pounce on any inadvertently dropped incriminating word he could frighten out of her.

"Not really," she said, looking down at her tightly clasped hands wedged between her knees. The last months before her father died had been full of silent anger and barely-contained resentment against Selena. "We had hoped my father would be happy when he married Selena, but she seemed dissatisfied from the beginning. Nothing seemed to be right for her after she moved in. I don't know what she thought her life here would be, but she made clear to all of us that it wasn't what she'd expected. I know Dad was disappointed, too. They didn't argue . . . exactly. When Vin and I were around, they just stopped talking." *How long is this going to continue? This chair makes me cold. I wish I had brought my jacket.*

Savarous changed the direction of his questions. "Do you know how she met Mr. Lovato? We understand she was spending a lot of time with him."

Angela was becoming annoyed with this man, his abrasive attitude, and the subject of her stepmother. Did he have to go on and on about her? "Who knows? Maybe she originally met him through Owen Martin," she said. "Owen helped her with the funeral arrangements and all. Reynaldo was Owen's bookkeeper. My brother and I suspected Selena was seeing Reynaldo, had been seeing him, even before the boat accident that killed my father. Her running around with him didn't seem right, with dad just dying and all . . . " She didn't want to talk anymore.

"Do you think it's a romantic thing with her?" Savarous persisted.

Romance with Selena? Angela almost laughed. Selena didn't love anyone but herself. She only used people. "I doubt it. It's always money she wants. She thought my father made more with his charter service than he did. Knowing her, she's been looking for someone else who can show her a good time." All this conversation about Selena made Angela feel discouraged.

"Did Mr. Lovato think it was love?" Savarous asked, leaning forward. Had he been a hunting dog his ears would be up, his nose twitching, his tail straight out behind him.

"How should I know? I'm not a mind reader," Angela said. "You'll need to ask her when she returns." Angela fought the temptation to slide her chair back and away from the detective's relentless questioning.

"There have been indications that Mr. Lovato might have been associated with drug trafficking in Raven Creek. Do you know anything about that?"

She hesitated, trying to determine how much to say. Should she mention Selena's drugs? Drug trouble could turn into big problems for everyone once the police were involved. "I've heard talk that he might be a source. I don't know anything definite." Could Savarous pick up on her evasion? She hoped not.

"Can you tell me where you were Monday night?"

"Monday?" Angela had to stop and think. "After we left here, Kelly and I went to the Pizza Palace for dinner, then he took me home. Why?"

"Oh, we need to know where the people who knew Mr. Lovato were that evening. We're asking everyone." He added challengingly, "Does that bother you?"

"No." *What a nuisance the man is. Can he seriously see me killing Reynaldo, lifting him over a fence, and stuffing him into the coal conveyer?*

The detective seemed to have asked all the questions he wanted to, for the moment at least. The two men got up and shook hands with Angela as though what had just passed was only a friendly conversation. Savarous walked back to the work area with her. Spotting Kelly, he walked over to him and announced, "I've finished with Miss Tiedemann. Now we want to talk with you."

Angela gave Kelly a quick noncommittal smile, which seemed to worry rather than reassure him, and returned to the paint table.

Chapter Sixteen

Kelly accompanied Savarous and Winston to the recently-vacated chairs, wondering what they had said to Angela and what questions he could expect. When they were seated, Detective Savarous wasted no time in pleasantries. "Mr. Singleton, we are trying to find out where everyone who may have been involved with Mr. Lovato spent Monday night." He looked expectantly at Kelly, who returned the stare without speaking.

Was it a question or a statement? Kelly had decided he would reply when asked, but not talk more than absolutely necessary. Words could too easily be twisted to work against the speaker. He simply waited to hear what else the detective had to say.

Savarous, annoyance in his voice, said, "I asked where you were Monday night. Do you have a problem answering that?" His voice was demanding.

"Not at all," Kelly replied calmly. "After leaving here, Angela and I went to dinner at the Pizza Palace. We were there over an hour." He purposely took time with the answer. No way was he going to let this hulking detective hurry him. "Since we were both tired, I drove her home. We sat in my truck in front of her house and talked a few minutes before I walked her to her door. When she was inside I drove to my apartment, watched the news on TV, then went to bed. I slept until morning."

"Do you know anyone who could corroborate your not leaving your apartment again?" Savarous demanded. His feet were planted apart on the floor in front of his chair. He appeared ready to leap up should there be a need.

"No, I live alone. Besides, I had no reason to go out. I was tired."

Savarous's voice was slightly sarcastic as he said, "That's too bad. It would be helpful if someone could back up your claim." He paused.

Kelly looked blankly at him. Did he really expect a witness for someone who was sleeping? Crazy!

Then Savarous asked, "How well did you know Mr. Lovato?"

"Hardly at all. I knew he worked for Owen Martin, and I'd seen him around town occasionally. There was never any reason to talk to him."

"We know that you are very close to Miss Tiedemann. Did she talk about Mr. Lovato to you? I understand he was interested in her stepmother." Kelly was uncomfortably aware of the detective's penetrating gaze. "Didn't you sometimes meet him in their house?"

"We had better things to talk about than her step-mother and her possible romantic escapades. To answer your other question, I was seldom in the house," Kelly said carefully. "When Angela's father was alive, I spent more time there. Mr. Lovato would not have been present then. After Mr. Tiedemann's death, Angela and I met only briefly at her house, then we'd go out."

"Why was that?"

"Mrs. Tiedemann was upset over her husband being missing and later found dead. I didn't want to intrude. I'd always felt uncomfortable when she was there, so I'd stop in just long enough to pick up Angela. Then we would go someplace else."

"We've tried to talk to Mrs. Tiedemann, but haven't been able to reach her, so far. Do you, or Miss Tiedemann, know where she is?"

Kelly wondered why Savarous would think he'd know. He wasn't a member of the family. Then he wondered if Angela had been asked this question and what she had replied. "I haven't any idea," he said. "Angela told me today that Selena didn't come home last night. That's all I know." Angela had been concerned about Selena's absence, wondering if she was all right. Kelly thought Angela worried too much. Selena could take care of herself. If he had his way, he'd marry Angela, and she wouldn't ever have to think of Selena again.

Kelly was aware that Winston had been watching him, sometimes glancing at Savarous when a new idea was introduced. But he had given no evidence of wanting to ask anything or intrude in the conversation. His movements were limited to writing notes and occasionally adjusting his position on the inadequate metal chair.

"To get back to Mr. Lovato," Savarous continued. "Do you know if he was in anyway involved with drugs or smuggling? There's been talk of his having something to do with their distribution in town. What can you tell us about that?" The detective's tone was as much accusatory as questioning.

Kelly looked at him thoughtfully before answering. He didn't like bullies and this Savarous was definitely one. "As I said, I know almost nothing about him or his activities. There may have been some talk, but that's all it was. I'm not involved with that stuff."

"We understand you want to marry Miss. Tiedemann, but she is unwilling to set a date, wanting to clear her father's name of suspicion of drug smuggling first. Is that true?"

"She doesn't like some of the rumors she has heard around town," Kelly said, thinking that their wedding plans were none of this man's business. If Angela was determined to wait a while, that was her decision to make.

"So, if Mr. Lovato had used her father to import drugs, his death would remove a witness against Mr. Tiedemann and take away someone who could testify about illegal drug movement and his involvement? Isn't that true?"

Kelly wondered what the man was thinking. He certainly had a devious a mind. "I hadn't thought about it that way. Angela doesn't believe the rumors about her father, so Mr. Lovato's talking wouldn't have mattered. He could have said nothing of importance to her."

"You still might have thought you had reason to silence him. If he were out of the way, you would be able to marry the daughter. I can see a possible motive there for murder."

Is this man for real? Kelly stared at him. *What kind of mind would think of an idea like that?* He supposed the police lived in a different world, but this suggestion was bizarre. He leaned forward on the chair, intent on making his point. "Look, I don't know why you think I'd want to hurt a man I hardly knew. I love Angela, but I'm not about to go around killing people who just might possibly have some distant connection to her father."

Savarous said in a silky tone, "Oh, I don't know. If Mr. Lovato were supplying drugs to anyone in the family, you might believe you had to step in—protect them from harm." His voice was suggestive. He was presenting murder as a public service, as something that wouldn't be so awful if done in a good cause.

Murder as a virtuous act had no appeal for Kelly. "I am unaware of Mr. Lovato or anyone else supplying drugs to a family member," he said, speaking slowly and clearly. "But if I knew he was providing drugs, I would call you guys, not take the law into my own hands. That would be crazy."

"Murder to protect someone has been done before now. Perhaps you thought silencing Mr. Lovato would make you a hero in Miss. Tiedemann's eyes," Savarous offered.

Kelly had heard stories of police intimidating people into confessing to crimes they hadn't committed. *Does this arrogant man think he can scare me with his wild scenarios or lull me with platitudes? He'd better think up another strategy than this. He's way off the mark and insulting besides.* Forcing himself to look at Savarous with composure, Kelly said, "I think this has gone on long enough. I was willing to answer questions, but I'm not willing to sit here while you go fishing for theories." Kelly stood abruptly, nodded to Winston, and sent a look of distain at Savarous, then turned and with his head high and back straight, walked away.

He heard Savarous say as he stalked off, "I don't like him. I can usually get people to talk more freely. This guy was too careful."

Kelly glanced around, as Winston, tucking his notebook away, concurred. "Maybe we just need to give him more time to worry. He's a cool customer, all right."

CHAPTER SEVENTEEN

Kira smiled when she gazed out the open side door of the terminal. The sun had finally come out and flashed brightly off the waves in the bay. Eagles on the lookout for fish flapped overhead. Gulls rested along the dock railings, or squabbled with incoming birds that wanted perching space. She turned back from the door as Jackie, who also must have been looking out and been tempted by the improved weather, switched on the overhead lights. Blinking from the sudden brilliance, everyone looked up and smiled when Jackie declared a long lunch break, saying they should take the extra time to enjoy the good weather while it was here. Winter, with its gray days and rainy gloom, would be coming soon enough.

Susan turned off the projector and stepped back from its improvised support, a long board laid across the steps of two ladders. She straightened her back, rubbed her eyes, looked around the work area, and said, "Sounds like a good idea to me."

Kira was storing markers when Angela and Kelly, holding hands and carrying jackets, stopped to ask if it would be all right for them to take the afternoon off. They said the police questioning had been unnerving, and they needed time to get away, think, and talk. Kira instantly agreed, knowing it would be okay with Jackie, who had previously commented on Angela and Kelly's subdued demeanor after the interviews.

To Kira's surprise, Angela asked if she would be willing to stop by her house that evening, as Selena's long absence worried her. Kira was hesitant to interfere in a family matter. It was really none of her business. She was in Alaska as an artist, not a therapist, detective, or attorney. Later, thinking back on her decision, she was not quite sure what had made her give in to the request—perhaps it was Angela's stunned expression after the police questioning. In the past, Kira had known others who'd been grilled by the police. She was aware of the psychic damage that could be inflicted upon innocent people.

"I don't know exactly what I can do." Kira said reluctantly. "I'll admit that since coming here, I've become very concerned about what is happening in town . . . and its effect on you. Okay, I'll come tonight. We can talk about the situation, and I'll help if I can."

Kira believed Angela liked and trusted her. The girl might be hoping an outsider would see things in a new way, help untangle the muddle of their situation. It was undoubtedly a mess and getting worse by the day. Kira felt she could at least listen and perhaps give some support . . . but not advice. She didn't believe in telling others what to do, or how to handle their lives. They arranged to meet at Angela's house around seven o'clock.

Later, as Kira and Jackie walked out of the terminal, Jackie said, "I'll call Warren and ask if he wants to join us, at least for lunch. I think he can be tempted by food. Just don't expect him to go shopping with us later." After she called, Jackie reported that Warren would meet them in twenty minutes.

During the drive to the Panting Puffin, Kira was impressed by the number of boats parked in people's front yards: fishing boats, sailboats, and silver inflatable ones that, Jackie said, were called Zodiacs. As they reached the commercial center, Jackie said, "Many Raven Creek stores close for the winter, especially those that cater to tourists. This is a good week to shop the end-of-season sales. Clothes are often half-price, souvenirs the same. The locals don't buy a lot of items marked 'Raven Creek, Alaska', so they are the best bargains. Last year I found a wonderful jacket that was just my size. The gift shops are fun, too."

"Maybe I can do my Christmas shopping while I'm here," Kira said enthusiastically, looking at the "sale" signs in the shop windows as they drove down the street. "Alaska-made items would be unique, different from what I can find in Arizona. Do we shop first or eat?"

"Eat," Jackie said with determination, making a U-turn in the middle of the block to snag a parking place that had just opened in front of the restaurant. "I'm hungry and Warren should be here any minute."

Jackie was already walking toward the restaurant when Kira got out of the car. "Don't you want to lock the doors?" Kira called.

Looking surprised, Jackie said, "This is a small town. We don't need to lock up. Besides, what could be taken—work clothes, water bottles, trash? Don't worry. This isn't metropolitan Phoenix."

They walked into the Panting Puffin. Kira hadn't had a good chance to wander around the first time she'd been there. Now, inspecting the store's wide range of jewelry, colorful note cards, and calendars, all designed by Alaskan artists, she had a difficult time keeping her choices to a reasonable number. When Warren came in, she quickly paid for her cards, promising herself that she would return another day when time was not so limited.

At the food counter, they decided among the various soups and sandwiches offered, then found seats in the dining area. Warren asked, "How did the project go today? Are your people able to concentrate on their work, or are they still distracted by the coalyard mystery?"

"Things were going smoothly until the police came to talk with Angela and Kelly late this morning," Kira reported. "After their arrival, Reynaldo's death became the center of conversation again. I think everyone wanted to question Angela or Kelly about what the officers had asked, but hesitated to do so. They didn't want to pry."

"I decided it was time to give everyone a break," Jackie added. "That's why we're here early and why you were invited to join us." She smiled and leaned to pat Warren's hand. "We're right on schedule with the copying of Kira's design, so why not take some time off?" Jackie hooked her jacket over the back of her chair. "Something interesting happened this morning. Angela asked Kira to come by her house this evening, and Kira agreed to go. I was surprised at first, but now I think it may be a good idea. At the least she'll give Angela moral support. Maybe they'll be able to think of something that will help clarify the confusion about the two deaths—I mean Jason's and Reynaldo's."

"It's too bad that Reynaldo's death brings up the question of smuggling again," Kira said. "That's bound to be a sensitive subject with Angela and Vin. I hate to see them being sucked once more into drug rumors. Judging from comments I've heard, the town's people still seem of two minds about the *Halibut Hunter* and what it was doing on its last trip. Now, with Selena known to be seeing Reynaldo just before he died and not coming home last night, plus the rumor of his possible drug involvement, it will be even harder for those kids."

Warren said, "She may have returned by now. I'll admit I'm curious. Does Selena know something or, worse yet, is she involved in what happened to Reynaldo? Maybe, if she's at the house when you go, you can ask her. I wonder if she'll be willing to talk to you, or will indignantly tell you to mind your own business."

"She doesn't know me and would have every right to refuse to speak to me," Kira said. The little she'd seen of Selena with Reynaldo at Evan's restaurant made her think the woman would be a difficult person to deal with. "I don't believe silence is in her best interest. Her avoidance of the subject will give people ideas and arouse suspicions as to her involvement in this mess."

Hearing a familiar voice, Kira looked up. Owen Martin had come in by himself and was ordering at the counter. The friendly, good-natured expression that had made him so appealing to Kira when they'd first met at the terminal was absent and had been replaced by one that was dull and lackluster.

As Owen walked toward a corner table, Warren called out, "Owen, would you like to join us? We have room. No need to eat by yourself unless you want to."

Owen hesitated, then nodded. He pulled over a chair from a neighboring table to sit with them. "I guess I could use some company," he said. "I'm still sort of dazed. Who could have imagined something like this murder happening here in our town?"

"It's been a shock for all of us," Warren agreed. "Do the police have any ideas, or aren't they saying?"

"Judging from their attitude when they talked with me," Owen said, "I think they suspect everyone. They've already talked to me and to Angela and Kelly and who knows how many others? They did mention Reynaldo's possible drug connection. That seems unlikely to me. Although, after this, I'm beginning to wonder if I knew him as well as I thought I did."

"Would you have known if he were pushing drugs on the side?" Warren asked. "This town is a pretty blind to that sort of activity."

Owen sighed. "I don't know. I've been asking myself that very question ever since his death. He seemed to have an adequate income. I never thought of it as so large that it might be coming from anything but his work. Now, I'm beginning to wonder." He sighed again and looked sadly at Kira. "I'm going to miss his help in the office."

Jackie turned toward Warren. "Speaking of drugs, did you have a chance to question any of the students today?"

Owen looked up in surprise. "What's this? Have you been playing policeman?" It was the first show of energy Kira had seen in him since he'd joined them.

Warren smiled affectionately at Jackie. "I talked to a few of them. As I expected, they were very reluctant to say anything to me, especially since they had just heard about the murder. I don't know if Reynaldo's death frightened them or if it made no difference. I clearly felt that although they may like, even trust, me, there is a code of silence that most are reluctant to go against."

Jackie's face showed her disappointment. "Didn't they say anything that might help? Did they know anything about Jason?"

"One boy, Collin, had met Randy, the hand who was on the *Halibut Hunter*, but didn't know much about him. Collin saw him going onto Jason's boat one day, but had no idea why he was there. He had also seen him talking to some kids that he thinks use, but that was all he would say. Other students didn't seem very surprised when I hinted at possible rave parties. I couldn't get them to be specific about who, or where, and I was reluctant to push them to say more for fear of damaging my relationship with them."

"I think you were right to pull back," Owen said. "They probably wouldn't have told you anything else and will respect you for not pushing. In the future they may be willing to share additional information."

"I suppose that could be true," Jackie said, "but I'm disappointed you didn't learn more." By common consent, when the food arrived, they dropped the topic. When they finished eating, Warren suggested he take Kira sightseeing. "She's been working too hard," he said. "She should take time to explore the Raven Creek area."

He mentioned a park outside of town where they could walk right up to a glacier. "Parten Glacier is worth the drive." He winked at Kira. "I think the tourist center has a brochure that tells about bears and what you should do if you meet one. After your description of what happened at the coal yard, I'm sure you'll want to read it."

Kira laughed. "I would like to see your glacier—there aren't any in Arizona—but I can do without another bear. That one was sufficient." She added, with emphasis, "I prefer to live where I am number one on the food chain."

"I doubt we will actually come across any," Warren reassured her, "although there is a chalkboard on the outside of the building where they record sightings, usually only one or two a day." Warren gave a teasing grin. "You just have to talk or sing. Then the bears will probably stay away."

"I will babble incessantly," Kira promised, returning his smile. "If you can stand that, I'm ready to go."

CHAPTER EIGHTEEN

As Warren drove his Land Cruiser through town toward Parten Glacier Park, Kira gazed out the windows, amazed by the variety of businesses that could thrive in such a small settlement. They passed a boat supply store, its windows full of equipment completely foreign to her landlocked experience, and a gravel yard with piles of stones dug from the nearby riverbed. Her artistic senses were delighted to see white gulls resting there in bright contrast to the black rock. A lumber company advertised meat-smoking equipment. A fish processor offered halibut, salmon, and other forms of seafood to visitors and locals. They passed an upscale motel and several unpretentious restaurants.

When the car turned up the road to the park, Kira commented on the gray silt-laden water running next to the road. "I've always thought mountain streams were clear, you know, where you can see the rocks and fish on the river bottom. The ones in the valley are like that. They are full of spawning salmon and the water is beautiful. Why is this one so different? It's almost opaque."

"The mountains here are granite," Warren replied. "This particular stream flows from under Parten Glacier." He looked out at the water running in graceful interlacing curves along the stony riverbed. "Stones get picked up and ground into small particles as the ice slowly slides across the rocky upper slopes. The rock flour, or dust, is eventually released into our streams. That's why they are cloudy. Even the dirt in our houses and on the streets is granite gray."

Warren identified the spruce, hemlock, alder, and cottonwood trees that grew thickly along the sides of the road. The trees were interrupted infrequently by small openings where campers and fishermen could park. Kira noticed a car parked at the side of the road in one of the little pull-offs and once spotted a yellow pop-up tent by the stream. Occasional rutted dirt roads disappeared into the trees. When Kira asked about them, Warren told her they led to homes hidden back in the woods. "You may think Raven Creek a small town. It is, compared to Anchorage or Phoenix. But there are more people living in the forest around here than you might guess."

The scenic drive relaxed Kira. Warren said it was near the end of the tourist season, so most park visitors were already heading south. When he stopped the car at an overlook to give her a first view of the glacier, she felt cloaked by the silence of the mountains. Except for the occasional call of a bird or the rustle of grasses disturbed by an infrequent breeze, the quiet was absolute. Across an expanse of gravel, the sun reflected off the white frozen mass of Parten Glacier. Water flowed from its base in small, winding streams, passing over a wide stretch of broken gray rocks.

"I expected bushes and trees next to the water, not a barren span of gravel," Kira said. "It looks like a moonscape."

"The glacier was once much closer to the road. It's been slowly retreating for years and recently it has begun to melt back much faster than ever before," Warren said, leaning against the wooden railing that surrounded the viewing area. "The plants take a long time to get a foothold in the rocks after the ice retreats. That's why those rocks at the base of the glacier remain exposed. As we near the ranger station in a few miles, you'll see several signs in the trees at the side of the road, showing where the ice used to reach—as far back as 1818." As they drove from the overlook and continued toward the park, Warren added, "It's a good feeding and hiding place for moose—and a bear or two."

"Oh, wonderful," she said caustically. An open graveled area where no bears could lurk unseen suddenly gained a lot of appeal.

They eventually parked in an almost deserted tree-lined lot. Walking to the park headquarters, they halted at a chalkboard on the front wall of the building. It announced three bear sightings that day. "That many already?" Kira exclaimed, immediately determined to make enough noise on the trail to the glacier to assure there would not be another sighting to record.

Inside the building they admired a diorama showing the changes in the extent of the ice cover. A nearby rack held pamphlets about the geology of the area, how to reduce fire danger, and as Warren had predicted, the different ways to react to black bears or grizzlies. After reading about the bears to be found in Alaska, Kira said, "I don't think I'll be able to remember whether to make myself big and bluff it out, or be very quiet and back away slowly. If I were suddenly faced with that startling choice, I would probably try to do both at the same time.

One pamphlet suggested a person could get within about one hundred meters of a black bear before it would be disturbed. Very interesting, Kira thought, but she had no intention of testing that theory. "Besides, I never carry a tape measure," she said, "and I'd want to know that the bear was, without any doubt, well fed and sound asleep." As they left the ranger station a sign outside advised people, when faced with a grizzly, to, "Stay still. If attacked, get down, cover your head and play dead." The sign concluded with the advice, "If they start to eat you, fight back."

The half-mile path to the glacier was paved and made walking easy. It abruptly ended at a wide, stony area, an outwash plain, crisscrossed by many runnels of water. Beyond that barren expanse the glacier loomed, its icy face reaching up forty or fifty feet. Kira saw huge crevasses where old blue compressed ice was exposed.

"I'd like to go closer, if we can traverse those runoffs without getting too wet," Kira suggested.

As they scrunched across the gravel and stepped over weavings of water, Warren glanced toward a grassy bank on the right. Three young men were reclining in the weeds, backs propped against a log bench. "I think I recognize those guys," he said. "I saw them when I was helping at the computer club. They're Vin's friends. Not interested in computers—or at least they aren't members of the club. I wonder why they're out here at this time of day. I would expect them to have jobs or be in school."

"They certainly aren't working now. Just lounging in the sun and smoking," Kira commented.

"I can guess what they are smoking, too," Warren added with disgust. "Do you smell what I smell? I caught a whiff of it when the breeze came from that direction. I bet it is 'roll your own and don't tell where you got it' type stuff."

"So . . . do you have your own ideas about where they did get it?" she asked.

"It's easy to find around here," Warren said. "I know it doesn't often come by mail. The State Police inspect for drugs and have dogs trained to sniff it out. Car or truck would be more likely. Are they just enjoying the day like the rest of us, or have they arranged with someone to buy or sell some of the stuff they're smoking? It is out of the way here, without many people to watch what they do, but it seems a long distance for buyers to come. They're members of the group that hangs out at Owen's boatyard. If they use or sell drugs, they could have met with Reynaldo out there." Warren paused, then said, "I should be fair. No one is yet sure that Reynaldo was a dealer, so I shouldn't believe what is, so far, just rumor." With a raised eyebrow and wicked smile he continued, "If Reynaldo was their supplier, those young men will soon be in a bind."

"Will you be able to talk with any of the teachers this week?"

"I can try, but they are so busy getting school started, they may not want to take the time right now." Warren gave a wry grin. "I'll probably have to do it next week or face Jackie's wrath."

They continued picking their way across the rivulets until they finally stood in front of the glacier. Several signs warned viewers to stand well back, as it was liable to calve unexpectedly. Kira pulled her jacket tightly around her for protection from the chilly katabatic wind coming off the ice. Warren said, "Glacier means 'ice on the move.' That's what makes them beautiful—and dangerous—at the same time."

"Incredible," she whispered. "From the road I had no idea the glacier would be so massive. And look at those gorgeous blue colors . . . I believed people were exaggerating when they told me about them. That black I see darkening some areas must be the granite dust you were telling me about. I hadn't thought of glaciers getting dirty." As they moved nearer she exclaimed, "You were right. I can hear the glacier ice crackle."

Although she wanted to get closer, Warren vetoed the idea. "I have no intention of digging you out from under a fallen ice block. How would I explain to Jackie that I had allowed her favorite artist to be squashed? A year ago they found a jacket emerging from the thawing base of the ice. They are still waiting for the unfortunate owner to melt out."

"Warren, those young men smoking pot back there reminded me of something I've been wanting to talk to you about. I've my doubts about Detective Savarous," Kira said. They were now wandering across the gravel in front of the glacier and no one was close enough to overhear their conversation. "Do you know anything about him? I've talked with several people he's interviewed. They all think he is awfully aggressive in his questioning. Is that normal with him?"

After a pause, while they stepped over a runnel, Warren said, "I've known him since we were in school. Even then he had the makings of a bully. I'll admit I was surprised when he joined the police. He was not a boy who'd always abided by rules, but I hoped he might he might have changed since then. After your question, I would guess he hadn't."

"Do you think he may still be unwilling to follow the rules he's supposed to enforce? Maybe he uses his questioning to disguise his real activities? I realize I may be suspecting him only because of what I've heard from those he's interrogated. What I know of him I don't like."

"I agree. He's easy to dislike. He's always been like that. Still, I don't like to think he has become a crooked cop. Are you suggesting he might be involved with what those young men were smoking?"

"I'd hate to believe he was causing people so much stress just to hide his own iniquities, but he might be turning a blind eye to drug activities or, even worse, be involved in supplying them."

Kira had stopped walking and turned to Warren. "He is in a perfect position, as a policeman, to know how to get the stuff in without being caught."

On the way back to the parking lot, Kira noticed that the three lounging young men were no longer there. She reverted to her concerns about what was happening in Raven Creek. "If Vin is home tonight when I see Angela, I might ask him about the guys we saw smoking. Or maybe Angela knows something. Any new ideas would be welcome if it helps solve the problems that have cropped up here this summer." The mystery of Jason's death was upsetting enough. The murder of Reynaldo doubly troubling. If Angela or Vin should turn out to be even remotely connected, they might be in real danger. She said, "I don't feel comfortable—I doubt anyone does—knowing a murderer is wandering around town."

As they got into the car, Warren asked, "How can the police hope to find the killer when they don't yet know why Reynaldo was killed? Maybe it was for a reason totally unrelated to drugs. The police may be on the wrong track."

CHAPTER NINETEEN

The fishing floats hanging from the tree at the front of the Tiedemann house were gray in the fading light when Kira arrived. The house looked forlorn on its untended lot, and the illumination from several windows was insufficient to make a convincing statement of welcome. In this part of town there was little traffic on the street. The only sounds to be heard came from the breeze off the bay as it wound its way through the evergreen trees, the evening cries of the gulls and ravens, and the buzzes and clicks of awakening night insects.

As she made her way through the gate and toward the front door, Kira heard low voices in conversation, interrupted once by a loud woman's voice. All sound stopped when she pressed the doorbell. After a pause, she heard light footsteps. Angela opened the door.

"Hi, Kira," she whispered, as she stepped back to let her visitor in. "Selena showed up a few hours ago. She's in her room right now." Angela seemed to be struggling to control her emotions.

Stepping into the small living area, Kira was instantly aware of tension in the room. Angela introduced her to Vin, telling him she had asked Kira to come and help make sense of their present situation. Vin said nothing. He sprawled in a big chair in the corner, holding a beer and glowering. The table next to him supported another unopened bottle.

"Hi, Vin," Kira said into the silence. "Angela's told me some of what's been happening."

He mumbled a sulky reply, "Yeah."

"I'm glad you're here," Angela said, seeming embarrassed by Vin's reception of their guest. "Vin and I were talking about

Reynaldo. We can't think of anything new that will explain his death. I hope the police will do something quickly."

Kira asked, "Has anything happened since we talked today at the terminal?"

Angela glanced at Vin, then said, "Selena and Vin have been, uh . . . discussing her recent disappearance."

Vin looked up angrily. "Hell, I asked the bitch where she'd been. She didn't like that. Told me to mind my own business." He snorted angrily. "Now she's in her room, brooding, I suppose." He took a long swallow from his bottle. "She refuses to admit that what she does is our business, too!" He thumped the bottle on the end table for emphasis and leaned forward. "Did you know Angela was questioned by the police today? Kelly, too? When Selena's activities bring in the police we have a right to know what she's been up to."

Kira had seated herself on the sofa during Vin's outburst. Now, she asked Angela, "Did Selena give any indication of what she'd been doing or where she'd been—out of town, perhaps, or staying with a friend?"

Angela glanced at Vin, then replied, "Of course we asked, but she wouldn't tell us anything. The police have been hounding us to tell them where she was. How could we when we didn't know? Now, Selena refuses to say a word about her actions." Angela turned to Kira, despair on her face. "It was strange. She seemed worried by our questions, not just annoyed. You know—nervous, even scared."

Turning to Vin, Kira asked. "Why would she be scared? Could she know something about Reynaldo's death, or at least have suspicions? She knew him pretty well, didn't she?"

Vin gulped his beer. "I haven't asked her. We know she's been hot for him since before Dad died." Vin sounded disgusted. "Reynaldo seemed to have money and be able to show her a good time. At first they were careful and tried to not be seen together— not easy to do in a small town like this. I suppose she didn't want to push her luck, and Dad's patience. After the *Halibut Hunter* went down, they stopped trying to hide what they were doing. The fuckin' bitch!"

"Keep your voice down, Vin," Angela implored. "She'll hear you."

"I don't care. Let her." He raised his hands in a gesture of distaste. "She knows what I think of her. I'll bet he was the one who gave her those drugs I found in the house. She's probably involved in Reynaldo's death, or at least suspects something. Serves her right if she's afraid now."

Angela glanced fleetingly at Kira, then quickly away.

Kira thought it probable that Angela and Vin had previously agreed to say nothing to anyone about Selena's drug stash, but Vin's anger had made him forget their resolution. Vin's comment came as no surprise, since Angela had mentioned Selena's drugs when they were sanding at the terminal. She did wonder, if that information were to get out to the police, would they come with their questions again? Probably yes.

To her brother, Angela pleaded, "Please, Vin, be fair. Even though you don't get along with her, she did tell you she had the money to pay for your computer classes. I don't know where she got it, but at least she is doing something for us."

Kira had heard of people wringing their hands but never seen it happen. Now, that was exactly what Angela was doing. Obviously, she was cast as the peacekeeper in this house—and it was definitely an uphill climb.

"Hell, she just wants me out of the house. My being here cramps her fuckin' style." Vin threw himself back in his chair and waved his bottle in anger.

"It's good that she found money for your classes," Kira said, trying to emphasize something positive, "but have you considered where it might have come from? If you don't mind my asking, what happened to the money your father left? Perhaps she decided to use some of that for your school fees." It was possible that Selena might not be as heartless as the kids believed.

Angela and Vin exchanged a long look, then Angela hesitantly suggested, "Dad said he couldn't pay for what Vin wanted. I don't see Selena being suddenly generous. I've been wondering . . . maybe Owen Martin decided to help. He's known Vin a long time. Vin was regularly at Owen's boatyard with his friends. And Owen was around a lot after Dad's death—helping with funeral plans, legal paperwork, and other stuff. Selena could have told him about Vin wanting to go to the tech school."

Vin gazed down at the floor and made circles in the dust with the toe of his shoe. "I guess that's possible. Owen could afford to do it . . . and I've known him a long time. I suppose I'll have to ask him." He looked up. "But what does my schooling have to do with Selena's disappearing and Reynaldo's death?"

They both looked at Kira. At the moment there didn't seem an obvious connection.

Tonight was not the first time Angela had mentioned Selena's drugs, and rumors from other sources had previously reached Kira's ears. Could drugs, not physical attraction or money, be the basis for Selena's involvement with Reynaldo? Their relationship might be more business than romance. Perhaps she wanted to take Reynaldo's place in the supply chain. Kira hadn't met Selena personally, although she had seen her that one time at Evan's Fish House. Selena's conversation with Reynaldo on that occasion had not appeared lover-like. It would have been better described as secretive, even slightly confrontational.

It was now that Kira thought to ask Angela, "You said the police wanted to know when Selena came home. She's here now. Have you called them?"

Before Angela could answer, Selena stalked into the small living room. She wore a stylish print blouse, tight skirt, gaudy gold-toned earrings with ruby glass in their centers, and high heels that clicked on the wood floor of the old house. In her hand was a lit cigarette that sent smoke fluttering erratically into the air as she gestured. "Talking about me are you?" she snapped. "Yes, I did get the money for you, you ungrateful shit. And no, it's no use asking me where it came from. That's my secret. As long as it gets you out of my life, that's all I want."

Angela broke in hastily, "Selena, this is Kira Logan. She's the artist that designed the mural this year, the one with Dad's boat in it."

Kira didn't know whether to be polite and shake hands, or just be quiet and stay out of the line of fire. She forced a smile, which disappeared quickly as Selena gave her a cold, disinterested look. Apparently dismissing Kira as not worth her attention, Selena turned abruptly back to Vin. "I'm going out for a while, so you can go on whining. And you, Angela, quit trying to wait until everything is perfect. Just marry your Kelly and get on with your life. Some questions will never have answers." Her voice clearly expressed her annoyance and impatience with Angela.

She dropped her cigarette on the floor and ground it out viciously with a polished shoe. She spun around, jerked a coat from the front closet and headed through the kitchen toward the backdoor. As she was leaving, they heard her say, "But I've got some questions and tonight I'm damn well going to get some answers!"

The squeak of the screen, followed by the slam of the closing backdoor, echoed in the silence of the house. A car engine started with a roar. The three in the living room looked speechlessly at each other. Finally Angela said softly, "I wonder where she's going? She seemed very . . . determined."

CHAPTER TWENTY

Kira was shocked by Selena's animosity toward Vin and Angela. An audience didn't seem to bother her or moderate her vitriol in the least. Why was Selena so angry? Did Reynaldo's death upset her or was it the loss of him as her lover—or perhaps, supplier?

Angela said softly, "I wonder where she's going? She seemed very . . . resolute."

Vin leaned back in his chair. Kira could see that the tension was slowly draining out of him. "Who knows?" he said. After a moment he added, "I wonder what she meant about getting some answers? About what—and who does she intend to ask?"

Mindful of the murder at the coal yard, Kira feared Selena's anger might lead her into real danger if she lashed out at the wrong person. She was clearly intent on going her own way and going it alone. Well, best of luck to her.

After Selena's dramatic departure, they reviewed the situation, starting in the early spring, when Jason's boat disappeared, to when his body eventually turned up in the bay. The kids talked of the town's suspicious attitude about his extended trip, Owen's kind assistance to Selena, Reynaldo's unsettling presence in their lives, his death, and now Selena's precipitous departure to "get some questions answered." Kira asked about the three young men seen at the glacier, but neither of the kids could ascribe a special meaning to their presence there. It was late when conversation ended.

By the time Kira left, they were all emotionally exhausted, and Selena had not come back. Angela said she planned to be at the terminal in the morning and would let Kira know if Selena came home and talked about where she had gone and why. Judging from Selena's attitude that evening, Kira thought it unlikely the woman would say anything—if she did return.

* * *

Jackie and Warren settled onto the sofa before a blazing fire, having agreed they were looking forward to a comfortable evening away from the distractions of the day. Before Warren became lost in his book, Jackie reached over, touched his hand, and said, "Now that we are alone, I wanted to ask if you found out anything else from the students that you didn't mention earlier today?"

Warren held his place with a finger. "I did try, but it was difficult to get much information—I warned you the kids probably wouldn't want to say anything to me about drugs, especially since the murder."

Jackie was determined not to let him get away with a one-sentence answer. "Come on, you must have learned something?"

Warren looked down at her, his affection clear on his face. "As he walked by me, one of the boys mumbled that there was something going on out at the boatyard," he said. "I wanted to pin him down to find out if he really knew anything definite, but he didn't stop. He just kept walking. I noticed his eyes darting around as though checking to be sure he wasn't seen talking to me. I didn't dare do anything that would call attention to us." He squeezed Jackie's hand. "I've thought about it all afternoon. I think he probably overheard conversations here and there in school but didn't know anything definite."

"I suppose something could have gone on out at the boathouse," Jackie speculated. "Reynaldo did work there occasionally. He could easily have kept it secret from Owen. Were you able to talk with any of the school staff?"

"Principal Peterson said he didn't know much that could help me untangle the situation. He is aware of the problem. Sometimes he's had to call parents of students he suspected were coming to school under the influence of drugs or alcohol. When he contacted them they usually made excuses for their kids—not enough sleep, working too hard, or some other barely plausible reason." Warren shook his head in frustration. "Peterson hesitates to call the police, although he would if he found someone peddling the stuff on school grounds. He feels the police can't do much. Even worse, they might overreact and turn a simple problem into a legal nightmare for the families. The school officials are in a difficult position, especially in a small town like this."

"I know how well small town people keep secrets," Jackie said, "but I'd think these deaths would scare the truth out of parents. It seems to be doing just the opposite."

* * *

Two hours later the fire was slowly dying when Kira arrived home in Jackie's car. When she came into the room, Jackie hurried to the kitchen to pour wine. Warren offered Kira a comfortable chair. With a deep sigh, Kira sat and accepted the drink.

Jackie again took her place beside Warren. "Your meeting with Angela and Vin lasted a long time. You must be beat. Were you able to help straighten out the situation, or don't you want to talk about it tonight?"

Kira sighed. "It's all a muddle. I feel sorry for them." She set her glass on the coffee table, then leaned back, her hands slack on the arms of the chair. "Their lives are so mixed up right now. It's hard to know what is important and what is only very distressing."

Warren asked, in a calm voice, "What can you tell us?"

"According to the kids, the police questioned them about their activities on Monday night. But I wonder, why them especially? Anyone could have decided to do away with Reynaldo. He didn't stand out in town. That, too, seems odd to me. Can a person really be that colorless?"

"Are you thinking of anyone in particular as his killer," Jackie asked, "or are you just hoping it is some villainous stranger?"

Kira laughed weakly. "Oh, a villainous stranger would be perfect. Lacking that, the murderer might be someone we don't even suspect yet. There must be many people around here who are angry with the drug trade in town. Perhaps a city father or a school counselor might be tempted to put an end to the situation—or possibly a religious fanatic. Then there are parents, teachers—anyone, in fact, that's closely involved with kids. It could be another competing drug dealer, or just a drug buy that went wrong. Apparently, Savarous hinted to the kids that he thought Kelly might be guilty."

Jackie exclaimed, "Kelly? They must be crazy."

Warren held up his hands. "Slow down, girl. At this rate everyone in town will have a motive."

Kira gazed into her glass, as though searching for enlightenment. Then, thoughtfully swirling the liquid, she continued, "Often the most difficult crimes to solve are those done by strangers on the spur of the moment. This could be one of those situations."

Warren looked perplexed. "I hadn't thought of it from that angle. An unsuspected stranger might pull it off. He would be taking quite a chance, though."

"You've had a wearing night," Jackie said, as Kira covered a yawn. "You must be exhausted. When you see Angela at the terminal tomorrow, she may be able to tell you something more about Selena and whether or not she came home. At least, I hope she can. After what you've said about this evening's debacle, I imagine it will be almost impossible for those kids to stay in the same house with her. I bet they won't be there much longer."

Kira drained her wine glass. "What a shame for a family to fall apart like this. I wish it could be different for them." Yawning again, she said, "I think I'd better call it a night. Maybe inspiration will come as I sleep." She picked up her glass and returned it to the kitchen.

Later, in her room, her last thought was, *if the police talk to Selena tomorrow, will they be able to make sense of all this?*

CHAPTER TWENTY-ONE

Thursday

After too many beers, Vin went to bed late and awoke in a lousy mood. In spite of everyone's best efforts to guess where Selena had gone and to understand or excuse her actions, the fact remained: She was causing everyone a lot of problems. Morning brought no change in his attitude.

He heard Angela moving around, preparing to go to the terminal. When she looked into his room to say goodbye, she said, "I hardly slept at all. I kept waking and listening for the sound of the car, but Selena never came back."

"You look like you had a hard night. I don't know why you care," Vin mumbled sleepily. "Neither of us can stand that wretched woman. Of course, if she doesn't come home," he added, "I may have trouble finding the money she offered to pay for my school. In fact, we may both have trouble finding enough money to live on. Selena never discussed the terms of Dad's will, and we didn't have the sense to pay attention when it was read."

Angela nodded her agreement, said she was due at the terminal, and quietly left.

Who should have control of the bankbook? Vin wondered. If the accounts were in Selena's name, they were screwed. Had his father been so blind to Selena's character that he would leave their future in her hands? He hoped not. They had been too upset over his death to pay proper attention when the lawyer was with them. Stupid! He would check with the lawyer . . . *what is his name* . . . and find out how much money they could expect. Hell, Selena may have been holding out on them and spending all their money. That would be just like her. He vowed to get moving and ask a few questions.

In spite of his good intentions, he went back to sleep as soon as Angela was out of the house. It was way too early to think about that stuff. He finally crawled out of bed around ten-something, when the phone rang. Answering, he became instantly annoyed. The police again. They were still trying to locate Selena. His replies to their questions were abrupt. As far as he was concerned police problems with Selena were not his problems, at least they shouldn't be.

After a shower and a late breakfast he would prefer to forget, Vin was preparing to leave the house, when the doorbell rang. Through a side window, he saw two men standing outside. *They look like police.* Probably bringing some kind of official trouble, he thought. Reluctantly giving up immediate plans to go out, he opened the door.

Detective Savarous introduced himself and Winston, then said, "We're here to talk about Selena Tiedemann and learn anything you know about Reynaldo's death. May we come in?"

Vin looked at them for a moment, debating his chances of keeping them out. Grudgingly, he stepped back from the door and watched them move confidently past him into the living room. He realized they must be the same ones who'd interviewed Angela at the terminal. She'd described them and warned about their questions.

In the living room, Vin purposely took his favorite, and the most comfortable, chair. Last night's empty beer bottles still decorated the end table. Savarous chose an upright armchair. Winston positioned himself on the worn sofa and took out his notebook.

Tightlipped, Vin waited for one of them to speak.

Savarous broke the silence. "I think you know about Reynaldo's death, and I know you are aware of our desire to talk to your mother."

"Stepmother," Vin corrected him, irritated. "Our mother died several years ago." Angela had told him of the detective's mistake about the relationship the day before. Couldn't this dumb cop listen?

"Stepmother, then," Savarous said indifferently. "Anyway, we want you to tell us what you know of her actions recently, especially where she has been when not here at night."

Vin looked long at him, reluctant to answer any question from this man, whom he had disliked on first sight. Savarous may have been trying to be polite, but Vin could see by his rigid posture that "polite" didn't come easily.

After waiting in vain for Vin to speak, Savarous continued, his voice sounding impatient, "So, tell us about Selena."

Vin took a deep breath. "I don't know where Selena has been, or what she has been up to. She doesn't tell us her plans, what she has done, or is going to do." He shrugged. "I have no idea where she was, or is, for that matter." Frustration with Selena was building in him again and made his aching head throb. "She came home for a few hours late yesterday, had some of her usual cutting words to say to Angela and me, then slammed out."

"We asked your sister to call us if she came home," Savarous said censoriously. "Did Selena say anything to indicate why she was leaving again so soon or where she was going?"

"She just grumbled something about getting some answers. She didn't mention what the questions were, or who she was going to ask. Under normal circumstances, I would expect her to be meeting Reynaldo. Of course, she can't do that anymore." He felt a twinge of cynical pleasure at being able to say that. Then all of the previous night's annoyance returned. He slid down in his chair, folding his arms defiantly.

Winston sat perfectly still, as though fearful of interrupting the flow of words. Savarous asked, "How did she sound? Was she angry, worried?"

"How would I know what was in her mind? She was rotten to both of us. I thought she was just being her usual disagreeable, vengeful self."

Savarous's eyes sharpened. "What was she disagreeable about?"

"The same old things. She said she never liked us—I don't think she even cared about my father, for that matter. She informed us that the sooner we were part of her past, the happier she would be." Anger had become his best defense against the hurt Selena inflicted. "She said she would send me to school to get me out of the house, and told Angela to get married. Just her usual loving remarks," he added sarcastically.

"So you were angry?"

"Of course, I was. I hate her guts!" He held his body rigid, his hands clenched into fists. "Until she moved in here, the three of us were getting along just fine. Then everything seemed to go wrong. She wasn't happy with her life here, wanted more money, wanted Dad to spend more time with her. And she wanted us to disappear. She wanted! She wanted!" His voice rose. "Then she somehow hooked up with Reynaldo. He had more money than Dad, and she seemed happy to help him spend it." Vin had their attention now. "I wouldn't be surprised if he was the one that supplied her with drugs." Resentment rushed through him like a shot of adrenaline.

"Drugs! What kind?" Savarous asked. Winston busily wrote in his notebook.

Vin suddenly realized he should have keep his mouth shut. His anger had overpowered his common sense. "Probably just marijuana," he said reluctantly, "although I have seen some white lumps of powder once or twice." He rubbed his cheek slowly, dragging out the information just to annoy Savarous. "She hid the stuff at the back of the pantry. It's not there now," he hastened to add, as the two officers appeared ready to leap from their seats. "I suppose she thought it safely out of sight in such an unlikely place. None of us likes to cook, so we had no reason to scrounge around on those shelves. I just happened to be looking for a snack in there one day and chanced upon her nasty little secret."

"Did your father know about this? Did you ever tell him?"

"I don't think he knew, and I certainly didn't tell him. He'd no reason to look in that closet. The kitchen is Selena's space," he said gleefully. Then thought, *Take that, Selena!*

"Are you sure she doesn't have any other drugs in the house right now?" Detective Savarous asked sharply, glancing at Winston. "It might help us connect some of the information we have about this Reynaldo. He's beginning to appear as something other than the fine, upstanding citizen people have been describing." There was a quiver of excitement in his voice.

"She hasn't kept any here since Dad disappeared, at least not in the kitchen. I've checked. I imagine she does . . . did . . . her drugs when she was out with Reynaldo. She's spent so much time with him recently, that she probably didn't need to bring the stuff home."

"Was she aware that you knew of her habit?"

"I never said anything, but she might have known. I figured it was her business. I also didn't want to get Dad upset. They were having problems enough, and his knowing would only make the situation worse."

Maybe he should have told his father, he thought. His dad might have thrown her out. As things turned out, he and Angela were now stuck with Selena. Not good. Well, it was too late at this point. He couldn't change the past.

"And you have no idea where she is today?" Savarous asked again.

"No, I don't. But wherever she is," Vin said, gazing blankly out the window, "I hope she stays there. She's no loss to us."

"Before we leave, would you show us the place you say she kept her stash?" Savarous asked.

The question brought Vin's attention back to the present. "Sure, why not?"

He led them to the kitchen. The two officers spent a long time inspecting the cupboard and seemed disappointed to find nothing but cans of soup, vegetables, and spaghetti sauce, mixed among boxes of dried, prepared foods, assorted cooking equipment, folded towels, and aprons. Vin expected them to want to hunt further and was surprised when they said they would need a search warrant to go over the rest of the house. They were "satisfied" for now. *Well, good for them.*

As the two men were leaving, Savarous ordered, "Let us know when she returns. We need to talk with her. Anything more we can learn about Mr. Lovato and his activities might help find his killer. Since you've said Selena knew him so well, it's important that we question her. I'll leave my business card." With his fat fingers, he dug one out of his shirt pocket and handed it to Vin. "It's important that you call us as soon as she returns," he added sternly.

Vin closed the front door behind them and watched through the window as the men drove away. He just might do what they asked. It was time Selena was made to account for herself. She would hate it . . . and he would enjoy watching her squirm.

CHAPTER TWENTY-TWO

"**G**ood heavens!" Kira exclaimed, as she and Jackie walked into the terminal. "Are we being invaded? Where did all these people come from?" She had expected to see a parking lot that was deserted except for the mural volunteers. Now, a crowd of people carried boxes and bundles into the building, moving around busily on missions she couldn't begin to guess.

"Did you forget?" Jackie laughed in mock reproach. "The music festival begins tomorrow evening. The folks are here to get the building and their assigned spaces arranged and decorated." Jackie seemed amused by her surprise. "This place may look ready for the festival crowd this weekend, but there is still a lot of equipment from the cruise lines' summer season that must be removed or repositioned. Some of the counters will be used to take tickets. Others will stock festival T-shirts and caps for sale. The extra furniture goes out on the dock in back for storage. There's a large fenced area that can be locked for security. See there." She pointed toward a large door open in the back wall. "The forklift is going out now with a load."

The slow pace of the previous days was no more. Ceiling lights were on throughout the terminal. Kira hoped Jackie knew a way to darken their particular working area. Too much light would dim the projection of the master drawing and make it difficult to copy the last mural images onto the few remaining boards.

Kira saw that Owen had arrived. He was smiling as he walked toward her. "Quite a change, isn't it? And what you see is just the beginning. By tomorrow night this place will be transformed." His grin, and the tone of his voice, indicated to her that he shared her obvious delight at the awakening of the terminal.

"The festival part of this weekend is suddenly starting to seem real," Kira said. "I can't wait to see everything in place and the terminal full. Do a lot of people come for this?"

He laughed. "You'll be surprised. Besides the Raven Creek residents, people come from many outlying areas to enjoy the music, food, and the opportunity to shop for gifts. It's a great chance to see friends and relatives living in distant settlements who seldom have a chance to visit."

She was pleased to see that Owen seemed more relaxed and cheerful than he had been at the Panting Puffin—although he still looked like he could use a few more hours of sleep. The increased terminal activity appeared to have an invigorating effect on him.

"I always like it when the pace starts to pick up," he said. "Tomorrow, when the volunteer painters for the mural are here and the final colors start to go on, you will really enjoy being a part of the transformation."

"I know you're in charge of the paint table this year," Kira said. "Sixteen different colors are a lot to keep organized. It sounds like a big job. I'd be concerned that careless volunteers might mix up the paint colors and make a mess."

Owen's smile slowly developed. "If I don't stay on top of the job, it can become chaotic. You've probably noticed we number the paint cans to coincide with the numbers on the various parts of your drawing. I label the can lids, too, to avoid mistakes. The paint gets drippy when people pour from the big containers into their individual plastic paint cups, especially early on when the cans are full. So, in the beginning, I do that job. Later on, I just hope for the best."

Jackie came over to suggest everyone get to work. "I don't see Angela or Kelly here, but everyone else is ready. I think we can start. Kira, there's a light switch over by that side door. If you'll turn it off, it should be dark enough in here to provide the contrast we need to copy the lines and finally get this part of the mural completed."

They had been working for more than an hour, when Angela arrived and came to where Kira stood. Judging from her unkempt appearance and late arrival, Kira thought she must have had a difficult night. Her hair needed combing, and there were dark smudges under her eyes. Her clothes looked as though chosen at random. "What's happened?" Kira asked.

Angela said, "Selena never came back. She's still missing."

"Oh, no! Not again."

"I got up several times in the night, thinking I'd heard her car, but I was mistaken." She put her hands to the sides of her face. "The police are so suspicious. Can they really think we would try to hide her or make excuses for her? They seem unwilling to believe we don't know where she is."

Kira put a steadying hand on her shoulder. "Have the police said anything more to you since you talked to them yesterday?"

"Vin just called to tell me they phoned him and later came to the house asking for her. He told them she'd been home for a short time last night, then gone out again. They weren't happy to hear that. I suppose I should have called them, but I didn't think of it until you said something. Then it was too late." Her hands tightly clasped before her, she added, "Why does she keep doing this to us?"

"She's not really doing it 'to you,' you know," Kira said, trying to soothe her. After their meeting at the Tiedemann home, it was clear to Kira that Selena had no interest in her two stepchildren and wouldn't inconvenience herself on their behalf. Any redeeming qualities she might possess were incredibly well hidden. "She's so single-minded and focused on what's important to her that she isn't thinking of you at all. I understand why you would be angry, but I think you're wrong to take it personally."

She gave Angela a hug. "She can't stay away forever. Cheer up. She'll come back eventually, and then maybe your questions will be answered. Just keep in mind that you are not responsible for whatever it is she's doing." Kira realized this was easy for her to say. She wasn't living with Selena.

While they were talking, the activity in the terminal increased. Ropes were laid across the terminal floor. Using some kind of foldable lift machine, a young man began to tie the rope ends high on the opposite side-supports of the roof, thus, suspending the line high above the large space.

Across the room two women emptied large plastic bags filled with colorful, unevenly dyed fabric. Spread out on the floor, the dozen or more sheets covered a sizeable area. To Kira's amazement, one of the women, using several extension cords, plugged a portable sewing machine into the wall, balanced the machine on a skateboard, rolled the contraption out between two of the large sheets, and began sewing them together. To avoid wrinkling the fabric, the woman had to constantly scoot backward to allow the sewing machine to do its job.

Kira turned to Jackie. "What is all that fabric for? It looks like leftovers from a hippie T-shirt factory."

"It does right now," Jackie said, with a laugh. "By tomorrow the wild colors will be transformed into a vision of the Northern Lights, and suspended overhead as the centerpiece of the music festival's decorations."

Kira had doubts about this promised magical transformation, but decided to withhold judgment.

The mural volunteers left for a quick lunch at a nearby deli, then returned to the terminal for the final push to finish tracing the mural outlines onto the boards. Some of the marking pens were dry, but the few remaining gave promise of lasting until the last line was drawn. Kira hoped the same might be said of the volunteers.

A forklift moved cumbersome platform sections to the far end of the terminal, where workers rapidly assembled them into a stage. A pile of electronic equipment added to the disorder. Five people stood talking and gesticulating in the center of the room, apparently critiquing the setting-up process that was underway. Then they walked toward the stage and the nearby stack of speakers, looking at the preparations in that area. Their actions made clear that a music festival without enough sound would be a disaster in their minds. Seeing all the speakers, Kira considered stopping by the hardware store in town to buy earplugs.

By the end of the day, the drawings on all the panels were finished, and the panels stacked against the walls awaiting paint. Every small area on each board was numbered to correspond to a paint color, making the mural, in effect, a giant paint-by-number project. Owen said the numbers would simplify the process for the volunteers coming on Friday and reduce the chance of their painting colors in inappropriate places.

As the projector and other items were being taken down and packed away, Jackie remarked that Angela had not returned for the afternoon session. "I hope she hasn't become so discouraged or upset by Selena's activities that she will not come back. I think being a part of this process has been good for her. I'd hate to see her quit just as the painting begins."

"She said she wanted to talk to Vin again," Kira reminded her. "He was very angry when I first arrived at their house last night, but seemed calmer when I left. I imagine she wants to find out if anything new has happened to change the situation, such as fresh information from the police or Selena. Then, too, Kelly had to work today. I'm sure Angela depends a lot on his support. She was probably just worried and a little lonely."

"I could throttle that Selena," Jackie fumed. "She has been nothing but trouble for the family since she came here. Jason made a big mistake marrying her. It would be a blessing if she didn't come back, but I suppose we can't be that lucky."

CHAPTER TWENTY-THREE

When Vin parked his car in the graveled area of the boatyard, he thought of the previous Saturday evening he'd spent here with his friends. Then it had been almost dark and nighttime quiet. He'd been looking forward to talking with the guys about Reynaldo's death and what it meant. His plans hadn't gone as expected. In fact, it had been a bummer. Until that night he hadn't noticed, or maybe not wanted to notice, how his friends had changed. Tory and Helmond were arrogant, plain unfriendly. The closeness of the group looked to be a thing of the past. He couldn't explain to himself when they began to seem different. He only knew he didn't like it.

Today, Owen's boatyard seemed a different place, bright from the sun reflecting off the glaciers on the hills behind it and shimmering off the water that surrounded it. The warm breeze carried the smell of evergreens mixed with that of salt water. It all reminded him of the many pleasurable hours he'd spent in this place during the long summer days of previous years.

He hoped to find some of the gang out here. They'd seemed more disagreeable recently, especially Tory and Helmond. He wondered why. He hesitated to think they were doing drugs, but their surly reception of him the other night was forcing him to consider that possibility.

He hoped, if drugs were being used, the guys might be willing to talk about their source. After all, they had been friends for years. Maybe, if he promised to keep their names out of it they would share some information that would help him find who was selling it. Then again, the breakup of the group may have progressed so far that he would learn nothing. At least he would ask.

He wandered out back of the workshop, where old boats waited to be repaired or to fall apart from harsh winter weather, neglect, and the passage of time. They were a sad-looking collection, he thought; paint peeling, rust growing, holes where there should be solid surfaces, and spare or worn out parts scattered around underneath the dying hulks. Today their appearance seemed in tune with his spirits.

He was in luck. He found Tory and Helmond lounging near a pile of timbers. Judging from the empty cans at their feet, Vin figured they'd been here for some time. He sauntered up to them, hands in pockets, casually looking around the area. "Hi, guys. I was hoping I might find you here. You've found a good spot."

Tory looked up, squinting into the sun. "It's you, is it? What're you doing here this early? Helmond and I are just passing the time. Isn't that right, Helmond?"

"Yeah. Just soaking up some of the last rays of summer," Helmod drawled from his sprawled position against one of the timbers. "Want a beer?"

"Yeah, sure," Vin said, settling on the ground beside Helmond. He took a can from the cooler, "I hoped you two might be around." He hesitated to begin. "The truth is, I need information and thought you guys might be able to supply it." *Will they even care about my problems?* Taking a deep breath, he plunged in. "Selena is missing again. The police are seriously looking for her—no luck so far. Angela and I don't know what to do. Selena was gone for a couple of days, came home for a few hours, and then barged out again. The police think we're hiding information."

"Those cops are stupid," Tory said. "Why do they want her? It's not against the law for a person to stay out overnight, or even disappear for a few days. Hell, I've done that plenty of times." He laughed raucously.

Vin continued, "You know about Reynaldo's death. Now the police are questioning anyone who might have known him. They've found out he and Selena were running around together. I can't believe she had anything to do with his murder—she couldn't have been the one to put him on the conveyer belt, she's not strong enough—but she may have known who was responsible."

"Now, there's a picture." Tory seemed to contemplate the idea for a moment. "Selena, in tight skirt and high heels, hoisting Reynaldo over the fence and carrying, or dragging, him over to where he was found." Helmond snickered.

Vin smiled weakly. "Be serious. I'm trying to figure out what's going on. Stop it if I can. This hassling of us by the police is getting out of control. I don't like having Angela mixed up in it. They questioned her and Kelly when they were helping at the terminal."

"So, what do you want us to do? Make the cops disappear?" Tory slugged Helmond lightheartedly on the shoulder, emphasizing his comment.

Vin wondered if these guys could ever be serious. "You talk to lots of people. You get around. Have you heard anything that would help me find Selena? More important, I need to know what you can tell me about Reynaldo."

Suddenly intent, Tory studied the label on his can. Finally, taking a long drink, he asked, "Why do you think we would know anything? Oh, we saw Reynaldo around all right, but why should we know anything about what he did or who would want to murder him?"

"I think you knew him better than you're saying. I think he may have been the go-to man for drugs." Vin tried to keep his voice calm. "Tory, I know you and Helmond use and have for a while, and I think Reynaldo was probably your source. He's dead now, so it shouldn't matter to you if I know. I need to learn more about him and where he got his supply. I'd also like to find out who else might have been in the business with him." Vin knew he had to be careful. If it sounded like he was pleading, his two friends would see that as weakness and laugh at him.

Tory and Helmond looked at each other but didn't speak. Vin could see by their tightly closed lips that neither wanted to discuss the subject, especially with him.

He took a deep breath and continued," I don't like being a suspect. The police may even think that my sister or I killed Reynaldo because of Selena. I've got to stop that. We don't care what Selena does on her own time, but the police don't seem to understand that."

"You don't want much, do you?" Helmond asked sarcastically. "Just enough to mess up our arrangements."

"Did the cops question you?" Tory asked.

"Yeah, just this morning," Vin replied. "They phoned early, trying to find Selena. She hadn't come home, and I couldn't tell them where to look. Later they came to the house to ask questions."

"What did you say? Did you tell them about her doing drugs?"

Vin didn't respond to Tory's question, hesitating to admit to what he'd said. He had hoped it was not common knowledge among his friends, but was quickly coming to realize that her habit was no secret.

"We're not blind," Helmond said, spreading his hands. "It was obvious to anyone who knows the signs. We thought it funny, your father acting so pure on the subject, and her chasing the leaves and white powder."

"It's not funny and right now she's causing us a lot of trouble." Vin found it difficult to remain calm in the face of their smart remarks. Helmond reached for another can from the cooler. Tory leaned back as though satisfied to bask in the autumn sun. It seemed that neither of them intended to say more. Before the silence lasted long enough to become permanent, Vin asked, "Can't you tell me anything?"

Finally, Tory spoke, questioning Vin for the second time, "Are you sure you haven't told anyone else about Selena's habit?"

"Who would I have told? I didn't mention it to anyone until a few hours ago. Kira Logan was at the house last night. She wanted to help Angela and me if she could. I got mad and said something about it then. Selena had been a real pain in the ass before she slammed out."

"You dummy. Kira will tell everyone," Tory's voice boomed.

"No, she won't. She's on our side."

In a voice of long suffering patience and growing suspicion, Tory asked again, "Who else have you told?"

Vin hesitated. This was not sounding too good. "Just the police. When they were at my house this morning, I mentioned it. By then I didn't care if it made trouble for Selena. She was really rotten to all of us last night."

Both guys looked at him as though he had lost his mind. In apparent disbelief, Helmond asked, "Just the police? Exactly what did you say to the cops?"

Vin, avoiding their eyes, looked at the ground in some embarrassment. He pulled up a small plant, examined it for a few moments, crushed it in his hands and threw it away. Looking out toward the bay, he said, "I told them we knew Selena had kept a stash in the house sometimes, but the situation changed when Dad died. After that, the stuff disappeared. We figured she was keeping it at Reynaldo's place since they were together so much." Looking back at his friends, he added with passion, "I have lots of ideas but no proof. I really need to know if Reynaldo supplied Selena, and maybe you guys, with drugs."

After a long pause Tory said, "You understand, we are not saying that we buy drugs, use, or know anything about them. However, if we did, Reynaldo might have been the man to know."

"Where do you think he got them?"

Helmond spoke up, saying, "Even if we knew, we wouldn't tell you. You might tell the police, then where would we be?"

Tory added, "Vin, you talk too much. We need to protect our supply . . . that is, if we have one, and I'm not saying we do." He winked at Helmond.

Vin felt he had no choice but to press on relentlessly. "The killer could have been someone who supplied Reynaldo. Or maybe it was a drug-buy gone wrong. Come on, guys, I need information." He took his time drinking his beer. This was too important to mess up now. "Did Reynaldo have any enemies angry enough to try to stop him? The killer could be someone we don't even suspect, a local do-gooder who wants to clean up the town. Or maybe Selena has a secret admirer. I don't know the straight of it, and it's driving me crazy."

Tory's attitude had changed. Now he frowned. His voice became harsh. "We can't help you. Your stepmother's problems aren't ours, and you're asking too fuckin' many questions. Just get off our backs!"

Vin raised his hands, trying to pacify them. "I thought we were friends. I was counting on your help."

"You want too fuckin' much," Helmond complained, in imitation of Tory, as he turned away.

"The cops have nothing for sure on you or Selena—maybe suspicions, but that's all," Tory said abruptly. "You didn't like Reynaldo and don't like Selena, so why do you, and why should we, care what happens to them?" He picked up his beer and took a long drink. "Forget it. Just be glad she doesn't hang around more than she does and make your life even worse. If you are lucky, with both Reynaldo and your father dead, she will pack up and leave—permanently. That will solve all your problems."

CHAPTER TWENTY-FOUR

Friday

Partially as a result of the unusually long daylight hours, Kira had become acutely aware of weather conditions since coming to Raven Creek. The sun's rays were slow to reach the house in the morning because the surrounding mountains intervened. Now the brightening sky, decorated by a few stray clouds, promised a nearly perfect fall day. Best of all, the time had arrived for the color to be applied to the mural. For Kira, it was sobering to realize how many months of preparation she, Jackie, and the mural committee had needed to produce this moment—the beginning of completion—so many small steps, so much behind-the-scenes work.

The first painting volunteers were scheduled to arrive at one o'clock. By then, the painting area would be completely set up and ready to go. Jackie had given Kira the responsibility of arranging the display table for the public. It would contain her original full color painting, the simplified outline drawing that had been projected onto the boards and copied, and a scrapbook with photos of previous murals. Also to be displayed was a computer illustration of the finished mural as it would appear on the side of the Manowin's store, plus a short historical information sheet Jackie had produced about the boats and ships in the painting.

"I think we can take our time," Jackie said during breakfast. "Nine-thirty or ten o'clock should be early enough to get to the terminal. Most preparations for today have already been made. Owen will take care of the paint table logistics. I just have to be sure there are enough supplies. When I checked yesterday, everything seemed to be in order. Don't let me forget to take the T-shirts with your painting printed on them to sell to the volunteers. I'll also need the sign-in book, to keep track of the volunteer hours. We have to justify our grant money."

"Will we have to provide snacks for the painters again?" Kira asked. "We don't want their energy to flag. I know I slow down when I haven't eaten for a while."

"No problem," Jackie reassured her. "Once the music festival is under way there will be plenty of food available: health food, junk food, ethnic food, whatever people want. No one will go hungry. Didn't you notice the eating area being set up next to the stage, in the back corner? By opening time there will be lots of tables and chairs there. They'll be needed. Cooking odors always attract a large crowd."

When Kira and Jackie arrived at the terminal the parking area near the front door was as crowded as the previous day, with people rapidly unloading vans and pickup trucks and carrying their bulky loads into the building. The crafts people were using carts to move their wares to their booths. Inside, the sales area was littered with boxes being unpacked. Drifts of wrinkled newspapers used for padding filled the aisles between booths. Kira watched with awe as ceramicists climbed on tall stepladders to install lights above their shelves, while their helpers carefully unwrapped handmade bowls, cups, and plates, and placed them for their best viewing advantage. Bead sellers were opening box after box of colorful inventory, arranging them on fabric-covered tables or hanging them in skeins from display frame hooks. The glass blower, his booth already set up, was filling the glass shelves over his workbench with examples of miniature animals and sailboats.

Kira wandered through the mounting confusion of preparations. The fabric she had seen being sewn with the skateboard-mounted sewing machine was now suspended high above the center of room. It was clipped to the ropes whose installation she had watched and wondered about. In spite of Jackie's assurances, she'd had doubts about the fabric's chance of resembling the Northern Lights. Now that the fabric was hanging it did indeed look like the Northern Lights—sort of. Kira also saw that the busy ladies had used more of their dyed fabric to construct a backdrop for the stage.

She returned to the painting area to check on the mural group's progress. A dividing rope had been set up to keep viewers from wandering among the busy painters. The public might not realize it until the damage was done, but it would be very easy for uninformed visitors to rub against the wet paint on the edges of the panels and come away with unwanted, colorful "racing stripes" on their clothes.

Nathan Barnes had been a constant helper throughout the week. Now, his red hair as unruly as ever, he helped Kira move a folding table to the front of the roped-off area. On this she arranged the photos, artwork, and data Jackie had brought from home. "What do you think, Nathan? Will the people take the time to look at all this information?"

He focused his bright eyes on her. "You'll be surprised. There's always lots of interest in what we do here." He squared up a scrapbook before continuing. "Remember, art and artists are considered just a little strange. And this year there is the added local debate about including the *Halibut Hunter* in the painting. People will pay attention, all right."

Nathan continued, "Let's hope people have stopped puzzling about Jason, his boat, or his possibly questionable activities. Attention now seems to have moved to Reynaldo. I don't know if that's good or bad. Whispers of his drug dealing are starting to circulate and the entire drug problem may move to center stage again. If that happens, we could find ourselves back debating again about Jason and our portrayal of the *Halibut Hunter.*"

Kira crossed to the paint table, where Jackie had joined Owen in checking the supplies. She could see he had been busy. Boxes of latex gloves were piled near the back of the table, rolls of paper towels were lined up next to them, buckets filled with water stood ready for soaking the foam brushes, while stirring sticks were mounded behind the paint cans. Plastic cups for the paint were stacked in several locations along the length of the table.

Glancing to the side of the painting area, Kira noticed Susan Gorman, who had previously been in charge of the projector. She was busy setting up her own small paint table. Nearby, a four-foot square white board lay propped horizontally about a foot off the floor. Moving closer, Kira saw it contained an outline drawing of two sea otters. Cut out and placed along the outer edges were smaller squares and rectangles.

"Hi, Susan, what are you up to over here?" Kira asked.

"Hello, Kira," Susan replied, straightening up from arranging floor cushions. "This is the children's mural. We do one every year. This will be displayed in the entrance to their school. The kids love working on it. And while they're busy here, their parents can wander the booths across the room and maybe buy a few items. Most of the families will come later tonight and this weekend. I intend to be ready before they arrive."

Looking again at the arrangement on the floor, Kira said, "I understand the sea otters, but why the geometric shapes around the edges?"

Susan smiled. "The music festival is a family celebration. We have children of all ages and skill-levels coming. The older ones will want to paint on the otters, the younger ones are not yet coordinated enough to stay within the lines. Besides, they like to make up their own decorations, so we give them a square of their own to work on. Surprisingly, once assembled, the parts always seem to work well together, as unlikely as that sounds."

Kira decided she'd wait to see the finished piece before offering an opinion.

While she'd been sidetracked with Susan, two roughly-dressed young men had come in and were talking to Owen. In spite of their clothes, Kira didn't believe they were volunteers. Looking closely, she recognized them as two of the three she and Warren had noticed smoking pot on her visit to Parten Glacier.

The young men and Owen stood at the far end of the table, out of hearing of the people milling around the supplies. She was not surprised when they moved farther off to the side. It was difficult to carry on a conversation as the number of people in the large echoing room increased. But was that their only reason? An intensity in their body language attracted Kira's attention. They appeared to be having some kind of argument, the young men wanting something, and Owen, judging from his frown and shaking head, disagreeing or putting them off. After a few minutes, the two turned away. They were glowering as they left the building. Owen wore a disgruntled expression when he watched them depart. Finally, he turned back to the table and began opening the paint cans.

Kira walked to where he stood and asked cheerfully, "Hi, Owen. Are you ready for the painters' onslaught?"

He glanced up quickly. "Oh, good morning, Kira. Are you excited about today? This year's T-shirts look great with your artwork on them," he added. "The volunteers will soon be daubing each other's shirts with the paint from the mural. Then you will see some real creativity." He paused, then continued, "To answer your question—I thought it time I began stirring. It always takes longer that I expect."

"Were those volunteers you were talking to a moment ago?" She was curious as to how he would answer the question. It was none of her business really, but she wondered about those particular guys showing up right now. They didn't seem to fit with the other people here, and their rapid departure aroused her suspicions.

Owen continued his paint mixing. "They had a question about the boatyard, that's all. I told them I was busy right now and would talk to them later. Young people always think their questions must be answered immediately. They have no patience." He scraped the stick on the edge of the can to clean off the paint, replaced the lid, rested the stick on top, then reached to open another can. "There are sixteen cans of paint to stir. This is my world today. The other part of my life can wait."

Kira looked at him closely. He seemed to be struggling to retain his old positive attitude. With Reynaldo's death and the police asking questions of everyone, she didn't see how he could avoid being distraught—this entire week had been overshadowed by the murder. After all, Reynaldo's body had been found practically outside the front door of the terminal.

"Well, you look like you'll be ready when the rush for paint begins," she assured him. "Jackie says you are the key person who keeps this process from breaking down." Kira smiled, then turned away, still not satisfied with his explanation of the two young men.

CHAPTER TWENTY-FIVE

The painting volunteers from town began arriving around one o'clock. Expecting to see high school and college "art school" types, Kira was surprised to find most of the volunteers in their thirties, forties, or even older—several much older. She reminded herself that these people were not coming from a big city talent pool and realized she had underestimated the wide appeal of a group activity in this remote country setting. This project provided people with socializing opportunities, while at the same time giving them a chance to beautify their surroundings. For those whose lives were focused on the ocean, the subject matter of this particular mural must be especially meaningful. Quite a few men were present, obviously old friends, judging by their easy interactions with each other. She concluded that this occasion was a small town "big event" . . . and kind of nice.

Jackie had once told her that most of the volunteers were experienced painters from previous years, so they needed very little instruction. Kira stood off to the side and listened as Jackie pointed to the small illustration of the mural on the information table and encouraged the volunteers to refer to it if they became confused. She also reminded them to not be stingy with the paint but to let it flow on freely, as the mural would have to stand up to the Alaska weather extremes when installed outside. She especially encouraged them to double-check their paint color number with the ones written in the spaces. Mistakes were easy to make and repainting took time. Since each board was only a part of the entire mural, it was easy for people to become confused.

Jackie had warned Kira that a few volunteers had no artistic ability at all. "They just come to be seen and to socialize. We have to bite our tongues until the untalented few have departed. Then it's time for damage control."

"Why do you let them paint at all?' she'd asked, bewildered.

"This is a community project," Jackie had replied. "It's more important that everyone support it than paint perfectly. Mistakes can be corrected when necessary. Peace first, perfection later. Then there are a few special needs neighbors in town who want to paint 'just a little space.' For them this is an exciting opportunity. They are always welcome."

A few minutes later Kira heard the last of Jackie's instructions to the volunteers and was introduced to them as the project's master artist. "I've brought these shirts you can buy and wear while you are here," Jackie told them. "Last year, painters decorated their shirts with artistic daubs of the various paint colors they were using. Their creativity was amazing. You can also ask Kira to sign them. I brought some indelible markers for that."

Soon, people had picked the color they wanted to apply and found the appropriate numbered sections on the boards. Most worked standing, leaning over to paint. Others, wilier or more experienced, commandeered the few stools and chairs that were scattered about, and settled down in relative comfort to fill their chosen sections.

Angela and Kelly worked together at a corner table. The board portraying the *Halibut Hunter* was hidden somewhere in the group of panels leaning against the wall, so they were filling in storm cloud and rain shapes on another one while waiting for an empty table to be available to hold the board that was important to them. Kelly occasionally joined with others to help move boards around. He lifted them with such ease that Kira realized he was stronger than she had thought when they met the first day of work.

She was relieved to see the two present and busy. Amidst all the turmoil in her life, it seemed that Angela resolutely clung to the belief that her father's death was unrelated to anything unlawful. Kira hoped that was the case, though she had to admit, if only to herself, that she had some doubts about his "accident."

Color number five was Kira's choice, a dark blue, to apply in a stormy water section. She walked to a nearby table where she found Nathan (gray-green, number eleven) and a tiny, fluffy-haired woman Kira had not met before (ocean-spray silver, number eight). The woman introduced herself as Millie, saying she worked part-time in a drugstore and "looked forward so much to adding my bit to the mural each year."

After carefully outlining her number eight shape, Millie said, "It's a shame people have been so mean about having Jason's boat in the picture. He was such a nice man, a hard worker, too. My husband thought a lot of him—them both being fishing people. What a shame he had to die like that—and then the fish and all eating at him. Makes me shiver just thinking about it. And now this other death . . . I say it's terrible." Looking across the board to Nathan, she gestured with her foam brush. "Why don't the police do something to stop all this?"

Nathan seemed to find Millie entertaining. "I'm sure they're working on it," he said, amusement in his voice. "What would you suggest they do, check for fingerprints in the entire coal yard, or perhaps line up everyone in town and give them the 'third degree'? I'd be surprised if there are any clues left on the conveyer belt where Reynaldo was found."

"Well!" Millie said, "I don't know about all the people in town, but they could question those that knew him. Someone must have ideas." She nodded to emphasize her pronouncement. "The police should check where all those people were Monday night. That's one of the first things they do in the police shows on TV, you know."

Obviously trying hard to control a laugh, Nathan said, "I suppose they've already questioned quite a few of his friends and acquaintances." Interrupting himself, he cautioned, "Be careful, you almost put your sleeve in the wet paint." He continued, "They haven't talked to me yet. Of course, I didn't know Reynaldo that well. I'm sure they've talked with his employer, Owen Martin."

Kira moved around the board to reach another section of dark blue. "I know they've questioned Owen," she murmured. "I wonder what he told them?"

"Well, he hasn't said anything to me about that," Nathan said, adding, "I saw him driving on Otter Bay Road that night as I was coming home from a friend's house."

"He's such a kind man," Millie said. "The local children have played at his boatyard for years. He's also a supporter of our sports teams, you know? Every town needs people like Owen."

"When I saw him he was going toward his boatyard," Nathan continued his line of thought as though Millie hadn't interrupted. Brush held high, he walked around the board for a better painting angle. "It seemed late for him to be out—Owen, I mean—but I figured he must have some extra work to do out there. Without Reynaldo to help him, he'll be keeping even longer hours."

"Nathan, I thought you would be collapsed at home after an exhausting stint working hard all day with us," Kira teased, "not out socializing at all hours." Concentrating on her work she added, not glancing at him, "You'd better keep your late night wandering tendencies a secret or the police will be speculating about what you were doing driving around at that time."

Nathan finished painting an edge. "I wasn't out long enough to be of interest to the police," he said tersely. Then, probably aware of the change in his voice, he said in a lighter manner, "You malign me unfairly."

"Only kidding," Kira assured him, surprised at the new tone in his voice. "It's just that everyone who knew or was a friend of Reynaldo is liable to be watched more closely. She put the final touch on a dark blue area, "There, that's finished. Now where can I find another number five shape that needs filling?" She picked up her paint cup, smiled at Millie, gave Nathan a thoughtful look, and turned away to find other panels with her number on them.

CHAPTER TWENTY-SIX

T he music festival opened to the general public at four o'clock. Kira noticed that young adults were prominent in the crowd, many easily noticed by their style of dress. They ranged from long-skirted, long-haired, tie-dyed wannabe hippies, to younger people experimenting with the "Goth" getups of dark lipstick, black clothes, and body piercings in the most unlikely, and probably painful, places. To balance all this sartorial excess, ordinarily-dressed multi-generational families were also present to hear the music and watch the dancing. They visited with friends, entertained their children in the play areas, or cruised the booths for gifts. The hungry ones sampled the exotic offerings that some of their neighbors were serving at the food booths.

It was difficult for Kira to remember this cruise terminal as she had first visited it, standing empty and dark, the air still, small sounds echoing. Now, with the music festival at full volume and the place filling with visitors, the space under the roof seemed to close in and vibrate with a painfully high level of noise. The dissonance of the electronic welcome greetings and the sounds of the bands emanating from the black speakers filled her head, leaving no place for rational thought. She felt assaulted by noise. Her only reality became the shapes on the board and the color she was painting. *I should have bought earplugs!* Other volunteers seemed to enjoy the confusion. This gave her hope that she too would soon adjust to the cacophony and it would eventually transform into music to her ears rather than into the permanent deafness she thought more likely.

At five-thirty Jackie came to where Kira was working and suggested it was time to eat. Kira suddenly realized why her painting had seemed to be going so slowly. She was starved. "Oh, yes," she said gratefully. "Now that you mention it, I'm more than ready. Let's ask if anyone else wants to come with us."

Owen and Nathan said they would join them as soon as they put their supplies away. The two women poured the extra paint from their cups back into the larger cans, cleaned their hands, and eagerly joined the crowd in the food court, where Jackie chose a curry dish and Kira ordered Indian fry bread. "I guess my stomach is still in Arizona," she said, when Jackie commented on her too-predictable choice. "Tomorrow I'll try something more challenging, although I'm not sure that curried rice is typical Alaskan food."

They found three places to sit at one of the long folding tables covered with white butcher paper. Jackie retrieved a fourth folding chair, so as to be ready when Owen and Nathan arrived.

Kira bit into her fry bread. The spicy mixture of beans, onions, tomatoes, and beef, on the fluffy bread, was wonderful. Just like at home. Soon the two men arrived with their food and everyone concentrated on eating—not that they could have done anything else. Conversation was almost impossible with the loud rhythmic dance music playing on the other side of the food-court railing. They watched a performance by children from a local dance school. When the set ended, talk was finally possible.

"How is your work going, Owen? Are you able to keep up with all the demands?" Kira asked. Several times she had noticed a distracted look on his face when she glanced over to where he was stationed with the paint supplies.

Looking up from his Southwest wrap, Owen replied, "I've been busy all right, working late without Reynaldo."

"I'm sorry. I meant, are you keeping up with the paint demands for the mural?"

"Oh, the mural," Owen said, "My mind keeps going back to what happened this week. Concentration is not my strong point right now. Yes, the paint table is still under control, and we haven't spilled much. I live in fear that someone may decide to stir the paint using the wrong paint stick and mess up the color, or worse, knock over a can. So far that hasn't happened."

A juicy hamburger had claimed Nathan's attention. Now, between bites, he said to Owen, "I've seen you out driving a couple of nights this week." Catsup dripped down the outside of his left hand. He wiped it off with a paper napkin. Picking up his food again, he continued, "How can you spend so much time here and then work late, too? I'd be exhausted. I'm not surprised you are having trouble keeping focused. You must be very busy indeed." He rotated the sandwich and took another bite.

Owen's lips tightened as he watched Nathan. "What were you doing out that you saw me?" Then, meeting the questioning looks on the three faces around him, he added, "I only wondered why Nathan would be so interested in my activities. I'm a busy person and often out at night, especially during this festival week. I have many things to do."

"Didn't mean to rile you, Owen," Nathan said. "I am impressed with your energy, that's all." He rubbed his hands with his napkin, wadded it up, and dropped it on his paper plate. "Forget it."

"I guess I'm tired. Sorry." Owen picked up his empty plate and, his folding chair scraping roughly on the concrete floor, stood to leave. "I'd better get back to my post before someone makes a mess in the cleanup buckets or all the brushes disappear."

Kira watched as he wove his way through the crowd to the trash bin, threw his plate in, and disappeared toward the mural area. At that moment, a group of Celtic dancers took the floor, and conversation again became impossible.

CHAPTER TWENTY-SEVEN

Saturday

The weather forecast had predicted clouds and possible rain, but the day was starting out sunny. Phil Walsh, port worker, arrived at the Harbor Master building at six in the morning. At that hour the dock was free of activity. Later, it would be crowded with groups boarding the fishing boats, and sightseers lined up for the Otter Bay cruises. Early as it was, his partner, Roberts, was already drinking his first coffee of the day. Phil knew better that to interrupt before the caffeine had done its magic with Roberts's attitude. He would check the list of jobs waiting for them and keep his mouth shut.

Now that fishing season was ending, the list of things to do wasn't as long as in the summer. Phil knew what the first order of business would be and was looking forward to it. The tide was in, and this job would take him and Roberts out on the bay in the harbor's Boston Whaler. He always enjoyed the trip. Too bad it was such a short one.

Even now, in September, the captains still brought back happy clients with boatloads of fish to be unloaded, photographed, cleaned, and prepared for shipping home. Each afternoon the fish-cleaning stations were crowded with proud customers surrounding waterproof-clothed captains busy gutting the fish caught that day. The edible parts to be saved were piled at the edge of the worktables. The heads, entrails, and fins were tossed down a central slot between the tables, to land in the gut barge moored under the dock.

Every few weeks during the busy season, Phil and Roberts used the Whaler to ferry the filled gut-barge across the bay—always accompanied by hungry seagulls, an occasional eagle, and sometimes, an opportunistic sea otter. They dumped the rotting fish parts where the outgoing tide could disperse them. It was a stinky, messy job. The decaying innards and prickly skeletons tended to stick together and glutinous pieces of refuse often had to be pried apart. Fortunately, the use of long gaff hooks did the job efficiently. After checking the load in the barge the previous evening, Roberts had reported that it was time for a dump run. The barge had filled up surprisingly fast in the last few days, an indication visiting sports fishermen must have gone home satisfied with their catches.

Finally caffeinated and talkative, Roberts joined Phil in the locker room, where the two men donned waterproofs and baseball caps, all essential equipment no matter what the weather. The seagulls had a habit of pooping freely on everything and everyone below them, in their excitement over the food delivery.

Out on the float, after checking fuel, oil, and needed equipment, Phil cast off the lines. Then Roberts maneuvered the seventy-five horsepower craft to the fish cleaning station.

Screening surrounded the space underneath the station. It had been installed to keep animals from getting into the barge and pulling out fish parts, which would foul the water near the bank. Although the tides came and went, there was not enough water movement this near the shore to adequately clear away the debris.

With the boat in position, Phil struggled to roll up the protective netting, free the barge, and float it into position at the side of the whaler. With the bumpers deployed and the barge firmly tied on, Roberts slowly worked the whaler away from the close confines of the dock space, past the rows of anchored boats and the occasional pulsing jelly fish, to the open waters of the bay.

This was the part of the job Phil most enjoyed. He leaned against the wall of the pilothouse, closed his eyes, and let the sun warm the morning chill from his body. The salt-scented breeze refreshed his spirits. The tide was turning, the waves minimal.

This would be a smooth twenty-minute ride. He felt fortunate to be out on the water, enjoying the moment and, best of all, being paid to be here. Work was hard to find in small towns. If he had not struck it lucky, he might have been forced to work on one of the commercial fishing ships, out many days at a time and in all kinds of weather. This job allowed him to avoid that hardship. *Ah, this is the life!*

As the engine slowed, he opened his eyes to admire the towering mountains and the sunlight reflecting from the water. They had arrived at the dump area. It was time to empty the barge and feed the gulls and other marine life. Hungry fish roiled the surface of the water while birds swooped low overhead, then spiraled up again, impatiently squawking at the men in the boat to get on with their breakfast service.

Phil slipped over the railing of the whaler onto the narrow walkway around the edge of the barge. Making his way to the back, he pulled the pin that held the screen gate closed at that end. Then he went forward to repeat the process at the front. Once the gates were swung out of the way, he signaled Roberts to start the whaler slowly moving forward, thus, forcing the seawater to flow through the barge and wash the entrails into the bay. Phil busied himself with the gaff hook, breaking up the more stubborn lumps of flesh to ease dispersal.

For several minutes he was occupied with loosening sticky piles of fish parts at the back of the barge. Once they were finally dislodged and floating out with the other refuse, he looked around for other impediments. An obstruction forward was restricting the flow. He thrust the gaff hook into the stubborn pile, pulled . . . then stared. Not believing his eyes, he blinked, and looked again. It was not fish parts, although the color was the same. It couldn't possibly be what he thought it was . . . could it? He saw long strands of auburn hair entangled in the slimy muck. He straightened abruptly and frantically signaled Roberts to cut the engine. His emphatic motioning finally prompted his partner to put the boat in neutral. Roberts stuck his head out the cabin door and asked the reason for this interruption of the routine.

Frantically, Phil gestured toward the front of the barge. Grabbing Roberts's jacket for emphasis, he pointed at the large pale lump in the pile of fish parts and exclaimed, "That's no fish!"

Roberts exclaimed, squinting from the glare, "Oh, my God!" He drew a deep breath. "Oh, my God!" he repeated. "We've got to get back." He looked again at the unexpected find, then ordered, "Phil, quick, close the screen gates. We don't want it to wash away. I'll get on the radio and report to the office. I don't know if this will be Coast Guard or police business. The boss can figure that out."

CHAPTER TWENTY-EIGHT

The ringing bell, coupled with insistent knocking on the door, roused Vin from a deep sleep. His thoughts were confused by drowsiness. He couldn't imagine who would make all that noise so early. *What time is it, anyway?* As the sounds continued he resentfully shouted, "Oh, for God's sake, go away!" He could hear Angela's voice from her bedroom asking who it was.

The noise downstairs continued, the pounding getting louder. "All right. I'm coming," he yelled impatiently. "I'm coming. Just wait a minute, will ya?" The bed squeaked as he rolled out of it. His bare feet slapping on the wooden floor, Vin stumbled down the stairs to the source of the racket.

Angrily, he yanked open the door to find Detective Savarous and, behind him, Officer Winston. "You again. What are you doing here now?" he asked, startled by their presence at this early hour. "I told you everything I know the last time you were here. And for your information we haven't seen Selena since Wednesday night. So, what do you want?"

"The situation has changed since we last talked," Savarous said. "We need to speak with you again." He stood close, his nearness implying a physical threat.

Unwillingly, Vin opened the door wider. Saying nothing, he nodded his head toward the living room. As the two men entered, Savarous asked, "Is your sister here? We'd like to see her, too."

As Vin was about to speak, Angela called over the railing, asking who it was. He told her to get dressed and come down. "It's the police . . . again," he called back.

They waited in silence. Vin, as usual, took the large chair in the corner, Savarous the straight-backed one, and Winston, the sofa, his ever-ready notebook once more in hand. As they waited, Vin became abnormally aware of long-ignored dust on the old furniture. Backlighted by the morning sun coming through a dirty window, it gave the furniture the appearance of having a furry coating. The wall clock, in the adjoining kitchen, ticked in cadence with his heart.

Angela finally hurried into the room and looked around at the three men. The policemen simply stared at her. Neither stood nor spoke when she came in. In the silence she settled herself in a small chair. Her uncombed hair announced that she had hastily dressed.

Savarous cleared his throat for attention then began, directing his comments to Vin. "When we visited you Thursday, you told us Selena had come home the previous evening and later gone out again. Is that right?"

"That's what I said."

"And you stand by what you said?"

"Of course." Vin glared at him.

"What did you do after she left?"

Vin resented his belligerent tone, but answered, "As I told to you last time, Kira Logan was here that night. We talked for another hour or so after Selena flounced out. What's this all about?"

"Did you both go straight to bed after Ms. Logan left?" Savarous persisted, ignoring the question.

"I think Angela went to bed." Vin looked at her with a raised eyebrow. "I was still pissed and went out for a while. I had to get away and let my anger cool." *I could take her evil words—but the way she talked to Angela—that was too much for me. Angela has always tried to think well of Selena, give her the benefit of the doubt. But the things that witch said to her . . . I sure did need to get out. If Selena had stayed, I'd have been tempted to strangle her.*

"Did you walk or drive?" Savarous appeared to be leading up to something, stalking an answer that would tell against the two or conflict with what they had previously said.

"I drove my car." Vin sat up straighter in his chair and demanded, "Is anything wrong with that?"

"By yourself?"

"Yes, by myself. I didn't want company." He resented the cop's questioning of the truth of what he said and wondered if now was the time for him to refuse to talk without an attorney present. He didn't know who to call, so he decided to go along with the interrogation for a few more minutes.

"Where did you go? Did you see anyone? Anyone that would recognize and remember you?"

"What is this?" Vin asked with growing uneasiness. Savarous only stared at him, saying nothing. Vin finally answered the question, "If you must know, I just drove around. I went out to the point and walked awhile. I was really angry and needed time to cool off. Eventually, I calmed down and came home. I was gone about an hour, more or less, and, no, I didn't see anyone. Besides, I couldn't have. It was dark by then. Now, exactly why are you asking all these weird questions?"

Savarous sent searching looks at both of them. "I said something had changed since our last talk. There has been a new development. Selena was located this morning."

"So? Where did you find her, and just why should we care?" Vin asked impatiently, as he thought, *You've found her, now you can keep her.* Then he saw Angela frown and grip the arm of the sofa. *There is something important Savarous has not told us. Why should he want to know what we did Wednesday night? Reynaldo was already dead by that time, and Selena had gone who-knows-where. What more does this cop hope to learn?*

Abruptly, Savarous leaned forward and said, "Because Selena was found early this morning . . . dead."

All sound in the room seemed to suddenly cease. Angela paled. Her hands were still clamped on the arms of the sofa. "Oh, no," she whispered.

Stunned, Vin felt the blood draining from his face, and his body freezing into immobility. He looked warningly at Angela, then asked the detective, "Where did it happen? Was it an accident with her car?"

Savarous pinned him with a scowl. "She didn't have an accident. She was murdered, then buried, naked, under cast-off fish parts in the gut barge at the dock."

With a strangled cry, Angela sprang from the sofa and bolted from the room. Sounds of her retching came from the bathroom.

"Damn you!" Vin shouted, his body flooded with indignation. "You didn't have to tell us that way. Do you like shocking people? What's wrong with you?" Outraged, he was having trouble subduing the flood of obscene words that rushed through his mind. He had an overwhelming urge to punch Savarous, but held back, knowing where that would get him—in more trouble.

He looked at Officer Winston, and thought he seemed uncomfortable, even surprised, by his partner's brutal approach. But the officer didn't speak, only concentrated on his notebook. *Why does he look surprised? Is there more behind the detective's words than meanness? Is his gruffness hiding an uncertainty or fear of something?*

Then Savarous spoke again, and Vin's mind returned to Selena's death. "The medical examiner says she was probably killed sometime Wednesday night or early Thursday morning." Savarous scowled at Vin. "He needs to perform an autopsy to be sure. It will give us an idea of when she ate her last meal."

Shaken by all that was being disclosed, Vin sank back into his chair, unable to speak. What was being described was so outrageous as to be almost unbelievable, disgusting, yet Savarous seemed to be enjoying himself. Vin wondered if that was what happened to some officers after too many years on the force? After a long pause, Vin asked, "What do you want from me? I still can't tell you anymore than I did Thursday."

"I want you to come down to the morgue and officially identify her body."

The noises in the bathroom had ceased by this time. Glancing toward the hall, Vin saw Angela had crept back to listen unseen, from the adjoining room.

"You mean you had the nerve to come here this morning and drop this horrible news on us, when you haven't even positively identified her yet?" His anger surfaced again. "I can't believe it," he said, throwing up his hands in disgust.

"A formality only. There's no doubt whose body it is." Savarous seemed to be watching him like a snake watches an approaching mouse. "We would like you to come with us . . . now."

Barely controlling his fury, Vin said, almost snarling, "I need to put on something other than these shorts I slept in, and check on how Angela is doing. After that, I suppose I'll have to come." With that, he levered himself out of the chair and stalked from the room.

On his way out, he overheard Savarous comment to Winston, "I wonder if the little shit is as shocked as he seems? I wouldn't put it past him to have been the one who killed her. He hated her enough to do it, and he can't account for his whereabouts that night. We'll talk to him some more when we finish at the morgue." Savarous paused, then added, "He should be ready to answer questions by that time."

CHAPTER TWENTY-NINE

On the drive to the terminal with Jackie, Kira looked ahead to the completion of the mural and wondered what interesting events the day would bring. The group painting yesterday had been far different from what she'd expected. She'd told Jackie that she'd originally assumed small towns would be filled with conservative, small-minded, boring people.

"Not so at all!" Jackie had exclaimed. "The people here are extraordinarily varied."

"I know that now," Kira had replied sheepishly. "So far I've met a psychic, a sled dog racer and a retired helicopter pilot. I think living up here and having to be so self-sufficient tends to amplify the unique qualities in people."

At the terminal they stowed their jackets behind the paint table with the coats and caps of other volunteers. While Jackie went to check the supplies for the day and confer with Owen, Kira walked from table to table to review the progress made on the mural the previous evening. She was impressed by the work already accomplished by this determined group of amateurs. Most of the painted sections were well done, though some would need another coat of paint. She speculated that the painters applying the paint too thinly must have been in a thrifty frame of mind.

They had been painting for some time before Kira realized that Angela and Kelly had not arrived. She was concerned, knowing Angela was determined to be an active volunteer and, especially, to be the one to paint her father's boat. Where could they be?

When her paint cup was empty, Kira went to get a refill. Owen looked even more tired than yesterday. Exhausted as he was, he was still handsome, and, she had to admit, brought out her care-giving instincts. While he was pouring the paint, she asked, "Owen, have you seen Angela this morning? I thought she would be here by now."

He put down the can and carefully replaced its lid. "No, although I'll confess I hadn't thought about it. I'm sure she intended to come. Maybe she just slept late." Owen looked as though he, too, should have slept in. His eyes were heavy and his skin lacked the healthy color present when Kira had first met him. She wished she had the right to put her arms around him and offer moral support.

Instead she asked, "Are you all right? You look done in. We need you here, but not so much that you make yourself sick." She looked for Jackie to back her up, but saw she was at the far side of the mural area. Kira continued, scanning his face, "I'm sure Jackie would understand if you wanted to take a break for a few hours."

His smile seemed forced. "That's kind of you, Kira, but I think I would rather go on working. I am a little tired, but I doubt I could rest if I went home. I might as well stay. I appreciate your concern." He paused, looking at her thoughtfully. "When this is all over I'd like to take you to dinner someplace where we can relax and get to know each other as friends, not just as fellow workers here at the terminal."

This was a pleasant development. Kira had hoped he might come to think of her as more than just a co-worker. "I would like that," she said. "Very much. Thank you." She cheerfully returned to her painting.

Sometime later she looked up to see Owen walking toward her. When he rested his hand on her shoulder, the serious expression on his face told her immediately that something new had happened. "What is it, Owen? Has something gone wrong?"

"Not wrong exactly," he said. "The police are here again and want to talk to me. I don't know why they can't wait until our lunch break, or after we finish today, but they insist that it be now. Could you stop what you are doing and watch the paint table for me? I'm uncomfortable leaving it unsupervised. I hope I won't be gone long."

"Owen, I'm so sorry." Kira put her hand on his arm.

She quickly collected her supplies and walked back to the table with Owen. The two officers she'd met the day of the bear-chase and the body-at-the-coal-yard were waiting.

*   *   *

"All right, gentlemen," Owen said, turning toward the two men. "I know of a small room that isn't being used. Shall we go there? That way, I won't be too far from here if I'm needed."

Savarous and Winston nodded their agreement and followed Owen to a long narrow storeroom. Pipes ran in and out of the ceiling and walls. Pieces of lumber were piled along one of the walls, boxes and folding chairs along two others. The only natural illumination came through the glass panel in the far door that opened to the outside. Officer Winston found the light switch and activated the two sixty watt bulbs. They unfolded three chairs and sat down.

Owen looked questioningly at the two men. "What is this all about? Have you found out any more about Reynaldo's death?"

Savarous studied him thoughtfully. "We've been investigating, looking around, asking questions, and decided it was time to talk to you again." He paused. "I understand you were out at your boatyard on Monday evening. Could you tell us what you were doing there?" His voice echoed in the barren room.

Annoyed, Owen said, "I don't know why what I did last Monday should be of interest. I suppose you've been talking to Nathan. He says he saw me driving home. I'd like to know what he was doing out that night." He looked from one face to the other. He didn't like Nathan's loose talk and his innuendoes. "Does he have an excuse for being out at that hour?"

"I can't tell you who gave us this information," Savarous said. "The question is, were you out there that night or not?" His determined tone of voice clearly indicated he would not be sidetracked.

"It's not unusual for me to go to the boatyard. I'd been working here all day and wanted to check on a project being done by one of my employees." Owen looked from one to the other of his listeners. "He was planning to use a new machine. I wanted to know how the work had progressed and if there were any problems."

"And had it gone well?"

"From what I could see, very well."

"So, what else did you do?"

"I read my mail, paid some bills, then checked to see that all the tools had been put away and the storage buildings locked. After that, I sat out by the water until I got chilled, then drove home."

"What time would that have been?"

"I have to think. I'm not sure. It was dark then. Maybe around eleven or eleven-thirty."

"You went right home?" Savarous persisted.

He nodded. "I considered picking up a snack somewhere but realized most places were closed, so I went home, made a sandwich, and went to bed."

Savarous glanced at Winston as though to be sure he was being impressed by his tough manner of asking for information. He waited for Winston to stop writing, then turned back to Owen. "Now, I need to ask you where you were on Wednesday evening. Were you out at your boatyard again?"

Puzzled, and suddenly wary, Owen looked at him and asked, "Why are you interested in what I was doing that night? Has something happened? What is all this?"

"Do you have a problem with answering my question?" Savarous retorted.

"Yes, I think I do." He regarded the detective steadily. "I'd like to know why you're asking it."

Savarous hesitated, sighed, and said, "This morning, Selena Tiedemann's body was found in the gut barge as it was being emptied."

"No!' Owen gasped. "You can't mean it." He could feel his face blanch and a sudden chill claim his body. *Who would have thought to look in the barge for her body?*

"The medical examiner estimated that she died sometime Wednesday night or early Thursday."

Owen knew Savarous was studying his reaction.

"We now need to find out where the people who knew her were during that period of time." He looked at Owen, his eyes unwavering, the muscles of his jaw flexing.

Owen said slowly, "Angela told me her stepmother would disappear for several nights at a time, telling no one where she went or whom she saw. She thought Selena might have stayed with someone here in Raven Creek, or Moose Pass, or even gone as far as Anchorage." He shrugged. "Anyone could have killed her, but why would they? And then to put her in the barge . . ."

"We believe her death may be somehow connected with Reynaldo's," Savarous said. "We are talking to everyone who might have had some knowledge of either victim."

"How did she die?" Owen asked. "She was full of life and planning so many changes, once the question of her husband's death was settled. And now . . . " He closed his eyes, but couldn't erase the vision of her body that sprang to his mind.

"Let's just say that, after her death, Selena was buried out of sight, deep under the fish parts, so no one would know she was there. Pretty clever of her killer," Savarous observed. His grin was wicked. "She was naked, so her skin blended with the other waste. Unfortunately for the killer, her body didn't wash out easily with the fish parts and disappear in the bay. She was found by one of the workers, when he tried to pry loose the pile of refuse holding her down."

Owen tensed. *Will Savarous never stop talking? The man seems to delight in describing that terrible scene.* "What do you want from me?" he finally asked. "I know nothing about this."

Savarous glanced briefly toward Winston, then said, "I want you to describe your movements on Wednesday after you left here. Did you go out to your boatyard again?"

"Wednesday . . . I think I picked up some food at the grocery store—a shrimp salad and some soup, as I remember—then I went to my boat in the harbor here in town, had a drink, and ate my dinner. I wanted to be alone. Reynaldo's death has been a personal blow as well as a business inconvenience. The confusion here at the terminal is hard on my nerves. I wanted some time alone. I was exhausted."

"Were you alone on the boat or did you have company?"

"As I said. I wanted some quiet time alone. I wanted to think."

Savarous was relentless. "People on a boat near yours thought they heard voices coming from your boat late in the evening—a woman's voice. Are you sure you didn't have company, someone you've forgotten to tell us about?"

"I told you, I was by myself," Owen repeated.

"Perhaps someone stopped by for a few minutes," he persisted. "Think back."

Owen closed his eyes, remembering that night. Suddenly, he looked up. "Now that you remind me, someone did come aboard for just a few minutes. I'd forgotten. But she was there for only a moment or two."

Savarous leaned toward him. "Who was it? What did she want at that hour?"

"As I recall, she was from another boat. She told me they had friends visiting unexpectedly and had run out of coffee. It was too late to drive into town. She wondered if I had some I could spare. I gave her what I had. That's all."

"What was her name? The name of the boat?"

"I didn't ask. I wanted to be alone, not start a conversation. I was worried about Reynaldo's death and the effect on my business. I'd gone to my boat seeking peace and time to think."

"We've been told an argument with some woman was heard."

"There was certainly no argument. There would have been no reason for one. If someone heard loud voices, they weren't coming from my boat."

"I think that satisfactorily explains everything—for now," Savarous said. Abruptly, he rose, gestured to Winston, and they departed.

It was several minutes before Owen came out of the room. He walked slowly, appearing to be in a trance. Finally, back at the paint table, he looked around as though he had never seen it before. When his gaze settled on Kira she gently asked, "Owen, are you all right? What did they want?"

Haltingly, he said, "I'm sorry. I've had a shock. I may be able to come back later today. Right now I need to leave. You'll have to take over here."

Without waiting for a reply, he retrieved his jacket, slowly fumbled his arms into the sleeves, and stumbled out of the terminal.

CHAPTER THIRTY

Vin entered the Tiedemann living room, still dazed from his visit to the morgue. He heard Angela and Kelly in the kitchen. Angela came rapidly to where he stood and hugged him. Kelly walked behind her carrying a cup of coffee, which he immediately handed to Vin.

Angela asked, concern evident in her voice, "Vin, you saw her?" She led him to his favorite chair, then she and Kelly settled side by side on the sofa. The three looked at each other. Silence descended over the small room. Finally, Angela asked, "Was it awful?"

Taking a deep breath, Vin spoke. "Not as bad as I expected, not like with Dad." He sipped his coffee. "But I'm glad you weren't there. It was Selena, no doubt about that. They must have cleaned her up after they took her from the barge. I was relieved . . . I don't think I could have managed looking at her covered with rotting fish parts." His voice trembled. *God, it was awful, not a sight for Angela.*

He was aware of the creaking of the old house as it adjusted to the rising outdoor temperature, and the whisper of tires on a car passing on the street outside. He rested his head on the back of the chair and languidly watched dust motes floating in the pale sunlight. Since Savarous first told them about Selena's death, the sun had moved and now came through the south-facing windows. It seemed an age since the man had been here.

Kelly asked, "What did the police say? Did they tell you anything new?"

Vin imagined that the two had been speculating about this since Kelly's arrival at the house following Angela's hurried call to him. They all wondered who Selena could have angered to the point of killing and disposing of her body in such a contemptuous way. Granted, she had constantly complained, been dissatisfied, and on the lookout for something better, not caring if her good fortune came at the expense of anyone else. She was heedless of other people's feelings and generally hard to like or live with. But murder . . .? It was more likely that acquaintances would simply avoid or ignore her. "The police aren't giving out much information on exactly how she was killed," Vin said, looking around the colorless room.

"After my identification of the body, we went to another room where they interrogated me, again." He picked up his cup of coffee and drank. The memory of that cross-examination haunted him. "Savarous was the worst. He wanted to know where I was from Wednesday night to Thursday morning. Did I know where Selena had been going Wednesday evening? Had I been jealous of Reynaldo—can you believe that one? He asked all kinds of stupid questions. Intimated I might have wanted to kill her, so she couldn't keep spending the money Dad left us. I guess I was starting to look like a good person to pin the crimes on. I'll admit, I was scared. They're probably feeling pushed to end these killings and find whoever is responsible. After this morning's ordeal, I've little confidence in the objectivity of the police when they think they are hot on the trail of their quarry."

"They must be crazy," Angela cried, jumping up to pace the room. "How could they think you would do something awful like that?"

Vin shrugged. "I should have expected it, I guess. When they came to the house Thursday, I told them that I'd gone out for a drive to cool off after what was said. The police are saying that I didn't leave to think—I left to kill Selena. I'd told them some of the rotten things she said to us that night. That was a mistake on my part." He slammed his fist on the arm of the chair. "How could I know she would turn up dead two days later?"

"I think the situation is getting out of control and possibly dangerous for us," Vin continued. "Until today, my contact with the police had led me to believe they wanted to help us. After today, it's obvious everything has changed. We can no longer consider the police to be caring public servants, but rather a pack of hunting dogs looking for prey. With Savarous in the chase, any victim will do. He won't be too particular."

Angela's eyes were bright with unshed tears. "I don't know where we'll get the money," she said, "but we had better talk to an attorney—fast—before this goes any further."

Vin agreed. "You're right. I was thinking of calling Dad's lawyer a couple of days ago, but couldn't remember his name. Now, with Selena's death, we need to know what's going on, as well as find out how to protect ourselves from the cops." After an instant, he added, "With Selena dead, we'll probably inherit everything. The police will think that's motive enough for us to kill her."

"Did they indicate they suspected anyone else but you?" Kelly asked. "There must be several people who could have done the murder." His somber words displayed his concern.

After a moment, Vin said, "It's my opinion that they believe the family is the obvious place to start looking when a crime like this is committed. They may want to question you again, Angela. I can't imagine they seriously suspect you. You're not strong enough to put Selena in the barge. Besides, why would you?"

Angela gasped.

"Come on now," Kelly exclaimed. "You can't mean they suspect Angela? It makes no more sense than suspecting you or me." Kelly reached to hold Angela's hand. "Don't the police have any brains?"

"You're asking the wrong person," Vin replied grimly. "I spent the morning talking to them at the station and now, more than ever, I can't explain their thoughts, or predict what they will do."

Continuing to discuss the possible future moves and questions of the police the three became increasingly aware that once started, and rightly or wrongly convinced of someone's guilt, the legal system could be a powerful force that would roll over all of them without doubts or remorse, and triumphantly produce a guilty verdict, with little concern as to the rightness of the decision. Sometimes innocence was an inadequate defense against misguided and unreasoning belief or inept police work.

"What will you say when the police ask where you were Wednesday night?" Vin asked Kelly as they discussed alibis. "Can you explain what you were doing . . . and prove it? All I could say was that I was out driving to think and calm down. They almost laughed at me. I hope you can do better than I did."

"Not much better, I'm afraid," Kelly replied in a dispirited voice. "I'd gone home, knowing Kira would be visiting you here that night. How can I prove I was by myself and stayed there all that time? How does one prove nothing?"

"Why would they suspect Kelly?" Angela asked indignantly. "He had no reason to hurt Selena."

"Oh, didn't he?" Vin snarled in a mixture of anger and despair. "The two of you have been going together for several years now. Everyone knows you won't marry until the mystery of Dad's death and the disappearance of the *Halibut Hunter* is solved. They might think Kelly was getting impatient with the waiting and decided to move things along. He may be slim, but he's strong enough to have done it."

His voice made it clear that he had no faith in the reasonableness of Savarous's thought patterns. He'd seen the tortuous paths the detective's mind could tread. "With Reynaldo, and now Selena, out of the way and my going to school, you would be living here alone. How much easier for Kelly to persuade you to marry him?"

Angela looked seriously at Kelly. "You wouldn't do such a thing . . . would you?" Then, probably realizing what she had said, she added quickly, "No, of course you wouldn't!" Turning toward Vin, she said, "You have a terrible mind. How can you say or think such things of Kelly?"

"It's not my mind that's terrible." By now he was pacing the room. "It's what I can imagine Savarous thinking. He wants someone to blame, and he isn't particular who it is. I think he'd do anything to provide a solution to these murders."

Angela raised her hands in incredulity. "He's supposed to be a detective. Doesn't he care about the facts?" Her voice held a mixture of disbelief and desperation.

Vin stopped his pacing and looked out the window. "He's a self-righteous blind ass in my opinion," he said. "He wants to solve the case fast and doesn't care who he hurts while doing it." He slapped his hands on the windowsill, then turned to face them. "He's not a detective looking for evidence to find the truth. He's an accuser on a power high."

"Whatever he is, he's dangerous," Kelly said. "If you want my advice, you'll both see that lawyer right away—today if possible." He paused. "Maybe I should, too." His voice was thoughtful. "I see hazards ahead for all of us, if we aren't extremely careful."

CHAPTER THIRTY-ONE

As Kira took over Owen's stirring and pouring job at the paint table, she thought of complaints she'd overheard about including the *Halibut Hunter* in the mural. Suddenly, one of the volunteers rushed into the room. "They've found another body! It's Selena Tiedemann. In the gut barge. Can you believe that? Of all places!"

The story made the rounds quickly. Kira saw the shocked faces around the nearby painting tables and realized that today would be another exercise in damage control. Drugs and the Tiedemann family would again be the focus of dissention regarding the presence of the boat in the mural. She immediately went to Jackie who was at a far table watching the volunteers. Apparently, she had not heard the news. "Jackie, we must talk."

Her attention captured, Jackie said, "Please, please, Kira. Don't tell me we're running short of paint. It's Saturday. The paint company could not prepare it, nor UPS deliver it, today."

"It isn't the paint. We're fine there," Kira reassured her. "It's about Selena."

"What has she done now?"

"Selena's dead. Her body was found in the harbor gut barge."

Jackie stared at Kira. "You can't be serious. Dead . . . and in the gut barge? Oh, my God. This will be horrible for the kids. Will the tragedies in that family never end?"

"I agree. It's awful."

Jackie repeated, "Those poor kids." She shook her head in bewilderment. "Angela once told me that Selena and Jason were not getting along well—but Jason is gone now. I can't imagine what Selena might have done to make a person hate her enough to want her out of their way—to kill her and treat her body with so little respect." She paused for a few moments, shaking her head. "I wonder why the gut barge?"

"That is bizarre, isn't it? It makes no sense unless the person wants a lot of publicity for the act." Kira stared into space for a moment, then said slowly, "They might be trying to frighten or send a message to someone. If that is so, I wonder for whom it is intended?"

"That's a horrible thought. A person would surely be crazy to use this method. And whoever would do that, would do anything. I don't like to think of someone like that running loose in Raven Creek." Jackie shuddered. "Who could it be? I don't feel I can trust anyone now."

She was quiet for some time, seeming lost in thought. "Let's talk about something else."

"I'm not sure my new topic will be any better, but it's something you need to know about. It's the controversy about the mural itself. Now with both Reynaldo and Selena's deaths, in addition to Jason's last spring, I'm hearing increased muttering both for and against including the boat. There's still plenty of sympathy for Angela and Vin, but I'm also hearing speculation about their possible involvement in the deaths." Kira dug her hands deep into the pockets of her work apron, her fists stretching the fabric. "Everyone is confused by what's going on in this town and concerned about what it all means." She looked out over the terminal, then continued, "You once mentioned you'd considered discussing the question of the inclusion of the boat with the members of the Mural Society, but feared that, if you asked for their opinions, they might easily succumb to the present uncertainty and vote to remove the *Halibut Hunter.*"

"Yes. When you and I discussed it, there seemed few good options," Jackie said. "Whatever course of action we chose involved risk."

"I hate even to suggest making any changes," Kira said, "But after what's happened today, I don't want your group to feel forced to keep the boat in the mural, and, thus, get into trouble with the town's people."

"I'm worried about the same thing, and haven't decided what to do," Jackie replied. You told me you wanted the mural to remain as planned, and I agreed. Selena's death does complicate things, but I'm still inclined to keep on with the work as planned and wait to see if the mural committee contacts me. This may be a case of 'letting sleeping dogs lie'."

The heated discussion earlier that week at the Panting Puffin was still fresh in Kira's mind. She cringed to contemplate what emotions would surface if they were to meet again. "If that's how you feel, I agree," she said. "Let's just go on as we are. If people are truly upset, we'll hear about it soon enough."

Kira had not expected Owen to return to the terminal and was surprised when he came to the paint table. His stunned look was gone, although she thought sorrow could still be seen in his eyes. "I came back because I had to," he told her. "Only a day and a half remains for the main work to be completed. I needed a break after this morning's events. I've had it, and now I'm again ready to help." He was still dressed in the attire appropriate to the clothes-endangering job at the paint table. "Thank you for taking over, Kira."

"I can keep working." She put a comforting hand on his. "Should you be back so soon?" He was a nice person, she thought, and grieved over his being caught unaware by this violence.

Owen looked down at her. His expression offered appreciation for her concern. "Work will help keep my mind off the disasters of this week, Kira. Sitting alone, while restful for the body, did nothing to keep my mind from going in circles. I decided I'd rather be here doing something."

"Then thanks for coming back," she said. He did look better than he had after the police talked with him. "I could understand your wanting to leave after the police were here this morning. A session with them can ruin anyone's day."

"That's the truth," he said, with strong feeling. "Hearing details about the finding of Selena's body was bad enough. Then they asked about rumors she'd been on my boat just before she disappeared. I was stunned." He slammed his fist on the paint table. "Here, I've been helping her and her family get their paperwork and finances in order . . . and now the police have the gall to suspect me of her death! Me? How could they?"

"They probably have to ask all kinds of questions," Kira said, trying to soothe him. "I'm certain they couldn't really suspect you of being involved in such an awful act."

A wry grin appeared on his face. "Thanks. I appreciate your confidence. I suppose I just let them get to me too much. That Savarous is such a creep." He shook his head.

"Let's talk of other things," Kira said. "Since you left this morning, I've tried to keep the table as organized as you do, but I will admit, I'd rather be painting."

Owen smiled and nodded. "Okay. I'm ready to man the mess. Go ahead."

Hesitating no longer, Kira poured paint into a cup, snatched a foam paintbrush, and headed toward a nearby panel. She was within hearing range when Jackie approached Owen and said, "Welcome back. Having you here eases my mind." She looked at him intently. "How are you getting along?" This question seemed to include both the paint table and his mental health.

"I'm happy to be back in all the confusion again." Seemingly, he wanted to redirect the conversation away from himself. "Have people commented on how the work on the mural is coming?" He scanned the tables and the people busily bending over them. "You've made a lot of progress since I left this morning," he added.

"The passing public seems to like it. I've had to answer a lot of questions. Many don't read the information we put out on the table—sometimes I wonder why I bother," Jackie said. She beckoned Kira to join the conversation. "Kira and I have been wondering if we need to make adjustments in the images, specifically the image of the *Halibut Hunter*. She says there has been a lot of talk today among the painters. We've tentatively decided to wait and see if public opinion reaches critical mass. What do you think?"

Owen continued stirring paint. Finally, he said, "I'm in favor of waiting, just as you are. To change anything now might bring more attention than if we did nothing."

Jackie exhaled a deep breath and nodded her agreement.

The afternoon progressed with lots of talk eddying around the tables. It seemed more focused on gossip about Selena than discontent with the mural. Once, looking up, Kira noticed Kelly and Angela standing outside the ropes designed to keep onlookers out of the way and paint free. She joined Jackie to welcome them, saying, "Good to see you two. I wasn't sure you would be coming back to help. How are you . . . and Vin? Is there anything we can do for you?"

Angela's red-rimmed eyes seemed haunted. "Kelly and I can't work today . . . I couldn't. But I still want to paint Dad's boat and wondered when that would be happening. Tomorrow I hope. It's important . . ." Tears came to her eyes and she turned away.

Jackie reached over the dividing rope to hug her. "No one but you will do that part of the painting. I promise. We have to finish the panels on the tables first. The remaining unpainted ones will come out tomorrow, maybe late in the morning. Then the one with your dad's boat will be ready. Until then, you and Kelly don't need to be here. Go home, or take a walk on the beach. Whatever eases your hearts. Then come back Sunday. The painting will wait for you. Don't worry."

Angela nodded. With Kelly's arm protectively around her, they turned and walked out into the sunshine.

CHAPTER THIRTY-TWO

Sunday

Sunday morning arrived wrapped in layers of threatening gray clouds with tangled ribbons of mist streaming low on the sides of the mountains. In Kira's opinion, the elements were inauspicious for a music festival, or any other kind of celebration. The weather outside made staying indoors, sitting next to a fireplace, and reading a good mystery, the best choice for the day.

Riding with Jackie to the terminal, she cheered herself with expectations of finishing the remaining panels and seeing the pride of accomplishment the volunteers would feel. Contemplating all the colors in the mural, finally generated enthusiasm for the day. Colors, textures, and interesting shapes affected her that way. *Typical artist*, she thought, amused.

At the terminal, Jackie pulled into a space toward the end of the third row. "Sundays may start slowly, but the crowds pick up by noon. These cars probably belong to the people with craft and food booths. I trust we'll see some of our painters as well."

Most of the booths were lighted and occupied by people busily rearranging, to best advantage, their information packets or remaining items for sale. The building hummed with an undertone of optimism. It was clear that these Alaskans were not about to let a little wet weather, or another murder, dampen their spirits.

Owen had arrived and was busy opening cans and organizing equipment at the paint table. Kira spotted several volunteers already working industriously.

"Good morning, Owen," Jackie called as they walked into the mural area. "I'm happy to see you. Did you get a good night's sleep?"

"Yes, much better, thanks. Good morning, Kira. What do you think of our weather? One day it's sunny, the next it threatens rain—normal for Alaska. All these clouds should be good news for the indoor festival. Visitors prefer to be inside on a day like this."

"I hope you're right," Kira replied. "I see the volunteers are here in gratifying numbers."

"They are a reliable group on the whole," Jackie said, as she scanned the large room. "We should finish most of the mural today. What do you think?" she asked Owen.

Owen agreed, then gestured the length of the table. "The paint is holding out, no problems there, and we have plenty of helpers."

Looking around at the work already completed, Kira saw that many of the panels needed only one or two more spaces painted to be finished. Once that was done, the completed boards could be leaned against the wall and others put in their place.

"That's a relief!" exclaimed Jackie. "Don't forget. This evening we are all going to Evan's Fish House. I invited Angela and Kelly to join us. They weren't sure if they would come. I think Angela's painting of her father's boat concerns them. They don't know if it will make her happy or sad. I hope they can join us. I'll certainly be ready to sit down and celebrate this evening."

"You can be sure I'll be there," Owen said. "I'm looking forward to it." He smiled at Kira. "This has been quite a week. I'm glad it's almost over."

Kira tossed her rain gear on top of a pile of coats, filled a plastic cup with paint, chose a foam brush, and went to join Marty and Tom Engelmann, who were painting a sinking freighter in the middle of a stormy sea.

Marty looked up. "Can you imagine the size of the waves and how horrible the weather would have been to make a ship as big as this one go down? And the poor crew—what a miserable time they must have had in the driving rain and cold. Then, after all their efforts, nothing saved them. They all died. I tell you, the more I work on this mural, the less inclined I am to trust my life to anything that floats on water."

"As long as you aren't out in the kind of storm this ship was in, you're probably all right," Tom replied. "You must admit the scenery around here is magnificent, and often the best and only way to see it is from the water. Just be sure to check the weather first."

"Is the campground still busy or have your campers started to leave?" Kira asked

Tom paused, holding his brush over his cup to avoid drips. "We aren't as busy now as we were a month ago, but a few people still remain. We'll also be leaving soon. Judging from what the last visitors are saying, it's the beauty of the golden fall leaves that keeps them here. I imagine many of the tourists, the weather being so gray today, will come here to the festival instead of sightseeing."

"It's a chance for them to see another aspect of Raven Creek and perhaps even purchase a few last minute mementos before they leave for the winter," Marty added. "I've been urging them to come to this festival. It's quite a change from the peace and solitude of their camping."

"You're right about the change. There's neither peace nor solitude here," Kira exclaimed. "I've tried to adapt to the noise, but I can't decide if I'm getting into the spirit of things—or losing my hearing."

Later in the morning, she heard Don and Nathan talking as they inspected the boards still leaning against the walls. Nathan was not quite his usual, cheerful self, and Don was definitely upset about something. He complained about how the subject of the mural kept him thinking of the drug issue in town. "I get so angry when I think of those pushers exploiting the weaknesses of our kids—and making money from it. If I ever got my hands on the bastards, I'd murder them." The venom in Don's voice surprised Kira. She had thought him to be a mild, gentle person.

"Don, calm down," Nathan said. "You're letting this paint project get you too worked up. There's no proof that drugs come in by boat." Nathan looked alarmed as his friend's voice rose in volume.

"How else would the stuff come in?" Don asked sarcastically.

"Cars and planes," Nathan suggested, "maybe cruise ships." Then he added, "This mural is really getting to you, isn't it?"

Overhearing the exchange between the two men, Kira wondered if the answer to the recent deaths was concealed somewhere in this room of dedicated volunteers.

"Damn right it is!" Don shot back. "Okay, okay, I'll shut up," he replied, when Nathan expressed distress at his words. "But you can't keep me from thinking . . . and watching."

Shortly following this last exchange, Kelly approached them, requesting the board with the *Halibut Hunter* on it. After a few moments search through the unpainted boards stored against the wall, they found the one wanted, slid it out from behind the stack, and carried it to an empty table.

Holding hands, Angela and Kelly stood silently, contemplating the panel. It was only a painting, but it was clearly full of meaning for the two of them. So many tragedies had happened to Angela's family. The two must have wondered if the death of Selena was the last, or would their nightmare go on and on?

People gathered around them to begin filling in the numbered spaces. Kelly brought two cups of paint, handing one and a brush to Angela. Giving her a quick hug, he began painting a water shape around the boat. After a moment of hesitation, Angela sighed and bent to put color on a memory.

Kira, working at the table next to Don and Nathan, heard Don bring up the subject of the recent deaths. "I can't stop thinking about what's been happening in town this week. Two people dead, and neither by natural means."

Nathan, concentrating on painting an edge, took his time answering. "With Reynaldo, I might believe it was drug-related, simply because he seemed a secretive person. He might have had something to hide. Selena? I just don't know. If she were doing drugs, she could have known too much about the people involved in their distribution." He brushed a few more strokes. "I can't imagine she would be any danger to them."

"I know you think we should leave it to the police, but I have my doubts about them, too. If I'm aware that drugs come in, why aren't they?" Don gazed toward the front doors, as though remembering when the police had walked in. "I wouldn't be surprised if one of those officers is on the take. That Savarous now—he looks like a possibility."

"They probably do have suspects," Nathan replied. "We wouldn't know, because that information doesn't get into the paper, until they have enough evidence for an arrest."

"I suppose that's true." Don, continuing his painting, seemed deep in thought. Suddenly, he looked up. "The killer has been very creative about hiding the bodies. Have you considered that? There might be symbolic meaning in where they were found."

"Like what?" Nathan asked.

"Maybe using the coal conveyer for Reynaldo was meant as a warning to other drug dealers to get out of town. If I were working with Reynaldo, I would start to reconsider my options. Then there's Selena and the gut barge—the killer might be expressing his opinion of the whole nasty business of corrupting the kids here in town. If you put the two together, they send a strong message."

Kira had been listening with growing interest to the men's conversation. Now she said to Don, "That's an intriguing observation. Do you think it's possible? It would take a lot of planning by the killer."

"Yes, I do." Don nodded. "As for planning—consider where the bodies have been found."

Nathan looked at him with an expression of stupefied admiration. "Don, you come up with the wildest ideas. I would never have thought of that. You might even be right—a murderer with a social conscience. It's an interesting concept, but don't you think a warning in the local paper would have been easier. Something like, 'Take your drugs and take a hike. We don't want garbage like you here.' Much less work than killing people and hauling bodies around to symbolic locations."

Don straightened from his painting. "I'm serious. You have to admit that the two killings might make the suppliers think twice. I get furious every time I think about the promising kids in my classes who get conned into using crack, meth, or heroin, and lose their futures." He gestured with his brush, causing paint to splatter on the mural. "It's a dirty business. The suppliers deserve to be killed. Hanged, drawn and quartered would be good."

"I think many people would agree with you," Kira said.

"Come on, Don," Nathan said as he quickly removed the freshly dropped paint before it could dry. "Don't you think murder is too severe a punishment? Prisons are for people like that." Nathan seemed uncomfortable with the ferocity of Don's opinions. Kira was aware that he had known Don for many years, first as a student, then as his friend. This present outburst apparently showed a new aspect of his personality.

"Stealing years of life from kids can never be adequately punished," Don said vehemently. "Have you thought about who else in town might be involved in this madness?" He was waving his brush around again. "I've wondered about Owen. He could be mixed up in all this. After all, Reynaldo worked with him. And Owen has his boatyard. He could sneak the stuff in easily." He pointed at Nathan. "Remember, you saw him on the road the night Reynaldo's body was probably put on the conveyer."

"You can't be serious. Owen? He's too much of a town supporter to do anything like that. He's the last person I'd suspect." Nathan was adamant.

Through all their talk, Kira only listened, resisting the temptation to interject an occasional remark. She had no intention of getting into the argument or taking sides.

Still trying to distract Don from his growing tirade, Nathan continued adding color to the board. "You're thinking too much, Don." He straightened his back with a grunt. "Besides, we need to stop painting and put out new boards. Two have been finished while we've been working. Let's get moving."

"You're right, but I would like to ask Owen a few questions. I have my doubts about him."

Nathan spoke up quickly. "Don, for God's sake, keep your voice down. Suspicions aren't the same as proof. You could get in trouble with this talk."

A soft voice came over Don's shoulder. "Exactly what is it you want to ask me, Don?" Owen stood behind him, a cold look on his face. "You seem to have more opinions than facts."

Don's voice had become louder as his talk with Nathan progressed. Apparently, his words had reached Owen's ears. Although obviously surprised that Owen had heard him, Don hesitated only a moment before replying, "I'd like to know if Reynaldo was helping you with anything other that your boatyard business. I would also like to know what you were doing on the road so late Monday night." He turned to face Owen, his feet slightly apart, his hands balled into fists, his usual mild, understated personality disappearing as he confronted Owen.

Owen regarded him with barely concealed contempt. "Your curiosity about my activities baffles me. What I do and where I go is not your business. However, I can assure you that Reynaldo's work for me involved bookkeeping, nothing else. As for my being out driving, I was going home from my office at the boatyard after working late. I was minding my own affairs." He scowled at Don. "I would encourage you to do the same."

Don didn't appear ready to back down. "I've heard people saying that a woman's voice was heard on your boat the night Selena is said to have died. That might be of interest to the police." From what he'd said to Nathan, it should have been clear to all who heard his voice, that for him, the coincidences and his accompanying suspicions were beginning to mount alarmingly.

"The police have already asked me about that." Owen's voice held a note of triumph, as well as menace. "You're too late. I wonder why you're so anxious to put the guilt on me? Are you afraid the police may suspect you? I think you're a little too adamant on the subjects of drugs and dealers. Perhaps you decided to take matters into your own hands, protect your students, and save the world. What were you doing out at the time I was driving home? Perhaps the police should be asking you questions?" Though his voice was low, the stiffness in his stance and the rising color in his face proclaimed his anger. "I suggest you look to your own actions and motives and keep your inquisitive nose out of my business."

The two men looked intently at each other for a long moment, then Nathan broke the tension by reaching to slide out another board for the mural, as a reminder that there was still work to do. Owen abruptly turned back to the paint table.

Kira had been refilling her paint cup and heard the heated interchange. "Owen," she said, as he walked past her, "you two looked as though war was about to break out. Be careful. Don looked really angry. Do you think he might have anything to do with the murders?"

"Just a misunderstanding, I hope," Owen said. "He's probably feeling overprotective about his students and got carried away."

"I didn't realize you kept a boat on this side of the bay."

His tension visibly dissipating, he explained, "I use it for a little fishing and sightseeing with friends. It's not a very large one, although it does have two staterooms. For me it's primarily a 'getaway' from my business, when I feel the need. It's moored near the restaurant. Perhaps tonight, after dinner, we'll walk over, and I can show it to you."

Kira smiled. "I'd love to see it. I've wandered around the public floats here, but never been invited aboard any of the boats. Have Jackie and Warren seen it?"

"Several times. They probably won't want to come again, so I'll give you an exclusive tour. As small as it is, I think you'll be surprised by all the conveniences on it. If you have some free time next week, we'll go for a short cruise."

CHAPTER THIRTY-THREE

$\mathbf{A}$s the crowd grew, activity at the children's mural increased. Susan Gorman was kept busy helping the smallest ones control their paintbrushes. The older ones were able to work on their own. The children's play area, across the terminal, was also crowded. Kira noticed juggling was a favorite activity, along with learning to ride a unicycle, using Eskimo style yo-yos, and pulling on ropes to raise the trunk of the life-sized mammoth, making him bellow. Shoppers crowded the craft booths. Vendors of homemade soap, native carvings, bark containers, ceramics, and colorful glass beads were busy selling to the locals as well as to the tourists.

Curried rice, Indian fry bread, spicy chicken wings, and hamburgers rapidly disappeared down the throats of hungry visitors. Space to eat at the tables was hard to find. Frowning customers impatiently circled those who had finished eating and lingered to talk. The seating in front of the stage filled with people wanting to listen to the folk music, watch several belly-dancing groups, or marvel at the acrobats who climbed and twisted about on long streamers of cloth hung from the ceiling. The noise level was high, but only served to energize the crowd that had come to be entertained.

Kira wandered over to where Angela and Kelly were engrossed with their painting. "I see you've almost finished," she said. "Your dad's boat is looking good, Angela." She pointed to the figure of the boat. "Just one more color touch, and you're through. How are you feeling? Do you like it?"

"Mmm," Angela replied as she carefully finished painting a small area. She straightened up and took a step back to admire her work. "Yes, I like it. I'm relieved his boat is still in the painting. This is very important for me."

Kelly smiled and said to Kira, "I think this has helped settle some ghosts in her mind. It signifies public acceptance of her father by the community. She was worried that the people of Raven Creek might somehow prevent his boat being included. Now that uncertainty is over."

Suddenly, behind her, Kira heard a loud voice. "Public acceptance? I don't think so. Jason must have been one of that secret drug group that's brought these killings to Raven Creek. Don't forget, the murders were all connected to his family. What that girl's father has contributed to this community is death and drugs."

Kira whirled to search for the thoughtless person saying such things in Angela's hearing. Then she looked at Angela. Her face was pale, her eyes open wide in shock. Kelly wrapped his arm around her and led her to another group of painters.

Kira turned again to study the loud-voiced man. "Calm down, Doug!" said a man next to Loud Voice. "I never connected Jason with the drug business. He was a nice, hardworking guy."

The man named Doug continued, in a resentful tone, "I've supported this year's mural, even though the *Halibut Hunter* is in it, but I'll be damned if I'll get sad and blubbery over the feelings of the children of a drug-running captain."

Kira had not met the man. He glared at her, as though defying her to disagree with him. She considered saying something about unsubstantiated accusations, but realized that his closed mind had no room for new ideas. She chose instead to turn her back to him and simply walk away. The level of rage she'd heard in his voice had caught her unprepared. She'd not realized the extent of resentment some of the public still felt against Jason, or the connections being made about his death and the two murders that had taken place this week.

The last boards were now on the tables and surrounded by volunteers determined to complete the painting before the festival ended. Owen remained busy, pouring paint into cups, washing brushes, and supplying paper towels to the workers. Everyone knew what to do and was getting on with the work. Jackie was engrossed in painting a folding wave. Kira said, "I believe we are going to be finished in time. What a relief. I doubted we could accomplish this much when we began. It seemed such a monumental job."

"Amazing, isn't it?" Jackie replied. "Every year I wonder if we'll be able to pull it off, and every year the planning works out, and the people come through. I lose sleep over it, but at the same time, I love doing this. I must be nuts."

"Jackie, I just heard some intense grumbling about the *Halibut Hunter* being in the mural. I think you need to know of it—just in case."

Jackie looked up. "Who was complaining? No one's said anything to me."

"No, nor to me either. I thought the detractors had calmed down, until I heard those two men over there talking."

Kira indicated the two she had heard. Jackie said, "The short one on the right has volunteered here for several years. Doug is part-owner of the local laundry. The other . . . I don't recognize him."

"It was Doug I heard complain," Kira said, recalling the anger she'd felt on hearing his words. "I was surprised. I thought most of the resistance had subsided."

"Oh, dear." Jackie frowned. "I hope this doesn't mean he's part of a group that will insist on revising your design. I thought that once the painting was finished, the voices of dissent would disappear."

"I'm afraid those voices remain," Kira said, still speaking quietly. "However, as long as complaints remain a mumble, and don't grow into shouts, we should be okay."

By late afternoon, the crowd had tapered off. Some booths had run out of food and were closing. In the craft area, a few artisans quietly began to pack up, even though last minute buyers were still looking. The energy level, as well as the noise level in the building, had receded. The last entertainer sat strumming his guitar and singing in an uninspired voice. The children's area held only a few young ones listlessly swirling hula-hoops or bouncing balls.

Kira helped clean up the paint table, taking brushes to be rinsed and buckets of dirty water to be disposed of into the restroom. Returning to the main room, she talked to a few people who planned to return Monday to finish any touch-up painting that had to be done. They would also stack all the mural boards against the wall, put away the tables, and take up the plastic from the floor.

"We're going to Evan's in an hour," Jackie reminded those she had invited. "After today, we all deserve a good dinner. Owen, I know you'll be there. What about you, Angela? Will you and Kelly be joining us?"

Angela and Kelly stood off to one side. At Jackie's reminder of their invitation to join them for dinner, Angela smiled and said, "Thank you. Kelly and I will definitely be there."

"Good. We'll save places for you. You both worked hard. Now it's time to celebrate."

CHAPTER THIRTY-FOUR

W hen Kira and Jackie arrived at the house the rain was steadily falling. They found Warren reading in a chair by the window. On the table beside him rested wine, crackers, and cheese he'd prepared for the women's return after their long day at the terminal. The rich colors of the floor rugs made the room seem warm, in spite of the gray weather outside. Jackie and Kira greeted him before disappearing into their rooms to change from painting clothes into something more appropriate for dinner at Evan's.

When the women returned to the living room Warren put aside his paper and asked, "How did it go today? Is the big project finished?" He poured wine for them. "I thought you could use some of this before we go out."

"Thanks, Warren." Jackie chose a glass before settling onto the sofa. "We can't stay here long. Our reservation for dinner is in less than an hour." Leaning back into the cushions, she gave a long sigh. "It's been quite a week."

The fire in the fireplace temped all of them to stay home rather than go out into the rain. "This silence is wonderful," Kira said, with a deep sigh. "Two-plus days of loud noise at the terminal have been more than enough for me." She laughed. "All right," she conceded. "It may have been music to others . . . but it's been noise to me."

Warren, who had attended the music festival on previous years, sympathized with her, agreeing that the enormous terminal space amplified the sound to a disturbing degree. He asked, "Did the volunteers you needed show up today? I wondered if the weather would keep them away."

Jackie nodded, smiling. "You know Alaskans. A little rain won't stop them. We had plenty of help and finished painting all the sections of the mural. The volunteers came through again."

"I'm curious. Did Angela get to paint the *Halibut Hunter*? Since neither of you has said anything to the contrary, I take it that the boat remains in the picture."

"Yes, it's still in," Kira said, "and Angela painted it. I think everyone realized that she was the one who should do that. Kelly worked next to her, filling in ocean waves and offering moral support. When she finished, Angela seemed less tense. They will be with us tonight. You can judge for yourself."

"Good. That's one big hurdle overcome." He took a sip of his drink, then asked, "Anything else happen that I should know before we meet everyone at Evans?"

The gentle tapping of the rain on the windows had let up, and the room was quiet. "Nothing specific," Jackie said hesitantly, "except . . . there was a lot of talk today about these murders, mostly 'who did it and why.' Kira overheard one of the volunteers griping loudly in Angela's hearing about the *Halibut Hunter* still being in the mural. You know that Selena has been murdered, don't you?"

"Yes. It was on the radio. Rotten luck for the kids, for Selena, too, of course. The commentator also mentioned where she was found. Unbelievable."

Quiet descended on the room, as each of them seemed to consider the ramifications of Selena's death on the lives of her family and those who knew her. Kira said, from her relaxed position in her chair, "Jackie, were you close enough to hear when Owen had a run-in with Don?"

"They had a run-in? No, I missed that. What happened?"

"It was kind of nasty." Kira spoke slowly, as she described it. "In an increasingly loud voice, Don told Nathan he thought Owen could be involved with either the murders or the drug problems in town—maybe both. Owen overheard what Don said. For a moment I was afraid there might be a fight. You should have seen the look on Owen's face. As a teacher, Don is understandably upset about the effect drugs are having on his students. I guess today all his anger came out."

"You did have an interesting day," Warren observed, looking at the women. "I can't picture Owen deserving or putting up with that kind of talk. He's been involved with kids for years. Nothing has ever been said against him. Are other speculations going around I should be aware of?"

"Before the 'big confrontation,' I heard Don suggesting some of the police could be involved in the local drug trade," Kira went on. "He specifically mentioned that detective, Savarous. But, by then, I think Don was ready to suspect everyone. Later, someone else said he thought Vin had reasons to kill Reynaldo and Selena. In a way it makes sense. Those two caused a lot of problems for Vin and Angela. I just hope Vin didn't do the murders. Angela would be devastated."

Warren looked at his watch. "Enough of this lighthearted conversation. Let's get our coats on and go join some of the suspects and/or victims. This promises to be a jolly evening."

CHAPTER THIRTY-FIVE

Dan Evans, the owner of Evan's Fish House restaurant, stood at the door to welcome diners as they arrived. He obviously knew Warren and Jackie and greeted them effusively, asking them how they were and how the mural was progressing. "Your friends arrived a few minutes ago," Dan added. He led the way to their table, where the rest of the invited group was gathered.

With the pressure of finishing the mural behind them, everyone seemed lighthearted and ready to put aside the stresses of the previous week. After drinks were ordered, conversation began with what the people at the table were going to do with their free time, then veered toward things Kira should do before she left to go back "outside."

Kelly suggested hikes, even mountain climbing, if she were so inclined. "Just keep an eye out for moose," he warned her. "They're dangerous if you get between them and their babies. Moose may merely look like large deformed deer, but they will trample you if you get in their way. Mushers are wary on the trails in winter. Moose always have the right of way."

Tour boats and shopping were again highly recommended by Jackie. Turning to Kira she said, "After you have completed all these suggested activities, we can adjourn to the hot tub, relax our aching muscles, and watch the Northern Lights, if they oblige, although his is a little early for them. In a couple of months they will put on a spectacular show. All it takes is a sunspot or two, and a few days later, they really light up."

Picking up his fork as the salads were served, Owen reminded Kira of their plans to go out on the bay in his boat. "I'll show it to you after dinner," he said. "If the weather clears, we can take it out on Tuesday, after the final painting chores are completed. There's a fantastic place to eat on a nearby island. We'll go there for lunch. It's beautiful, and so peaceful."

Kira saw Warren and Jackie exchange a glance. She suspected they hoped Owen was developing an interest in her. He had been single for several years now. It probably seemed to them that it was time he found someone to share his interests.

Kira smiled at Owen. "Offer accepted with thanks." Then she added, "I've been surprised by how much work a determined group of amateurs can accomplish in such a short time. Raven Creek is full of talented and interesting characters. This entire experience has been fascinating."

Jackie laughed. "It's such a relief to have another mural finally finished. Frank and Sharon are eager to see it in place on the side of their store before winter sets in. I hope we can get it installed next week. It all depends on when we can get the equipment to lift the panels and the people to help fasten it to the building."

"Angela, you and Kelly did a fine job of painting Jason's boat," Jackie said. "He would have appreciated your love, and the courage it took for you to do that."

Angela patted Kelly's shoulder. "I had a lot of support from Kelly—from all of you," she added, looking around. She was thoughtful for a moment. "People became so distracted this week by the murders that the question of one boat in a painting almost became lost. I'm thankful for that."

Jackie spoke up. "I agree with you. The deaths did cast a shadow over the project. If the police came to the terminal one more time, I was going to hand them a paintbrush and tell them to get to work and quit interrupting."

Laughing, Warren put an arm around his wife. "I can just imagine you taking on the entire police department of Raven Creek! I wonder if Detective Savarous can paint or does he only excel in pointing fingers of suspicion at everyone he meets?" Everyone at the table laughed.

"I've wondered why he is so intent on treating each of us as his number one suspect," Owen said. "Is he trying to impress his superiors, or just hoping to scare everyone until someone breaks under the force of his beady eye?"

Kelly, leaning forward, added, "He's a friggin' bastard! He looked at me as though I were covered in blood. When he gave Angela a hard time, I could have slugged him. I'll never forgive him for that."

Angela put her hand over his. "With the deaths piling up like they are, it's not surprising he's desperate to find the person, or persons, responsible for those horrible acts. I don't like the way he's going about it, but I'm trying to comprehend why he's being so disagreeable. Perhaps, if I can understand him better, I may not feel so offended by what he says."

Warren smiled at Angela. "You are very wise for a young lady of your years. Trying to see the problems from another person's angle helps. Still, he's making it uncomfortable for everybody in town. I wish he would get on with it and solve these murders."

Over dessert, Owen said, "Enough of all this. I want to show Kira my boat. It's no ocean liner, but I've fixed it up comfortably." After slightly too long a pause, he added, "The rest of you are invited to come, too, of course."

Everyone at the table thanked him for the opportunity, but no one accepted his offer.

CHAPTER THIRTY-SIX

Outside the restaurant, Owen took Kira's hand as they walked down the ramp toward the docked boats. Feeling his warm, strong grasp, she looked up at him, and they shared smiles. The rain had not returned, the air was cool, and the odors of saltwater and fish swirled around them. Heavy clouds still hung above the bay, although scattered breaks in the overcast promised a chance of welcome sunshine by Monday. In Kira's opinion, there'd been more than enough rain, too many gray days, and too many deaths to plague her visit here. Now she wanted sunshine, so she could sightsee without an umbrella.

It was pleasant being with Owen. During the past week, she'd anticipated this evening with him more than she had expected. The strength of character he'd exhibited since Reynaldo's death had won her admiration and affection. She knew he'd struggled to keep going after the death of his employee and the dismaying actions of the police. Then the death of Selena had been announced. Following these catastrophes, the entire community was in a state of puzzlement and stress.

"I've been looking forward to this evening," Owen said. "When I'm busy at the office, I don't go out in my boat as much as I would like. With you here, I now have a good excuse to escape from work. I'm looking forward to our day on the bay."

Cheerfully, Kira said, "I am, too—and we'll be able to talk without raising our voices." In spite of his pleasant ways, he seemed lonely. Maybe they would develop mutual interests other than mural painting. She hoped so.

Once they stepped on the floats—Owen said they were called that because they went up and down with the tide, unlike docks that were stationary—the lights softly illuminated Owen's face and reflected gently off the still-wet walkways. "Going out on the water in your boat sounds wonderful," she said. "This area is so beautiful! I would love to see Raven Creek from the bay. And you also promised a great lunch. How could I resist an offer like that?"

Kira's growing affection for Owen made her steps unconsciously veer toward him. She found herself bumping against him when they walked—it was a little embarrassing. She realized she was becoming very fond of him. He was both warmhearted and confident—qualities she valued in a man. She had thought she would never again meet such a person, and in Alaska of all places, but here he was. She hadn't previously considered moving from Arizona, but for Owen . . . well, who knew what the future might hold? Tonight was just a beginning.

He led her past a group of sailboats, moored to the float, their masts like a slowly swaying forest of narrow white trees. A short distance past the sailboats, he pointed and said eagerly, "Here's my boat. I named her the *Raven Witch*. Come aboard and I'll show you around."

"*Raven Witch*. How did you come up with that mysterious name?" she asked. When he helped her on board, the rocking of the boat as it took their weight surprised Kira and momentarily distracted her from her question.

Owen laughed. "That seemed appropriate when I was naming her. She is docked in Raven Creek, and I anticipated her taking me to bewitching places—and so she has."

"Then I look forward to being enchanted when we go out later this week," Kira said. "Now, show me the inside of this beauty."

Owen fished a key from his pocket, unlocked the sliding door that gave entrance into the salon, and turned on the lights. Kira noted the carpeted floor in the salon area and flower- patterned cushions on the wicker chairs grouped around a glass table. She hadn't expected so inviting a space. Everything was extremely well-organized and neat. Now she understood the meaning of "shipshape."

Owen guided her on a short tour of the boat. The galley was a step up toward the front—called the "bow," Owen told her. Beyond that space was a large steering wheel, or helm, surrounded by a cluster of electronic equipment. Tucked under the counter was a raised chair suitable for the captain's comfort and convenience.

She was astounded by all the storage space that had been built into the most unlikely areas. The electronic equipment for navigation and fishing fascinated her. She'd had no idea so much information would be at the fingertips of boat owners. "I guess I've been lost in the age of Moby Dick," she admitted. "All these instruments you've shown me telling water depth and the location of rocks and fish . . . I'm impressed. After working on the mural showing so many nautical disasters, I'm relieved to find that boating is a lot safer than it used to be. Do you still use all those charts that captains used in the old movies, or is everything electronic now?"

With a laugh, Owen opened a cabinet door next to the wheel. "Some things are still necessary, or at least the Coast Guard thinks so," he said, pulling out several rolled up maps. He led her back to the salon and spread them on the small table. "Here, pull up a chair and take a look." Pointing to one of the charts, he said, "This one shows Otter Bay. Over here is the island where we are will go for lunch. As you can see by these numbers, charts tell direction, water depth, distance—lots of other things sensible people should know if they are going out on the water."

When she moved in her cushioned seat to get a better look at the chart, she felt something hard under her. Shifting her weight, she slid her hand down to find and remove the annoying item. Whatever it was had been almost invisible in the patterned fabric. She grasped the object, pulled it out, and then opened her hand to see what she'd been sitting on. Resting in her palm was a gaudy gold earring with ruby glass in the center. Its hanger was bent. *A strange thing to be lying about.* Then she felt a sudden shock. It looked exactly like one of the set Selena had worn Wednesday night when Kira visited Angela and Vin at their house. *How could one of those possibly be here?*

She straightened slowly, concealing the earring in her hand. While Owen continued to explain the information the charts contained, she stared at him instead of the charts.

Noticing her distraction, he asked, "Kira, what's wrong?"

Hesitantly, she said, "I wondered if I'd misunderstood you. Didn't you say Selena hadn't been on your boat recently?"

"That's what I said. The police asked if she had been here. Apparently, someone reported hearing me talking with a woman, even arguing. I told them a woman had come from another boat docked near me—she wanted to borrow coffee. But there was no disagreement, no loud voices. How could I argue with someone over coffee? Why do you ask?"

Kira slowly opened her hand. "How do you explain this?"

Owen stared at her, then slowly reached out to take the earring from her fingers. He turned it over several times, his expression that of a person seeing an unknown, otherworldly object he couldn't understand and would rather not touch. Taking a deep breath, he said, "I didn't notice the earring when I straightened up the cabin. I can't imagine where it came from, unless the woman off the other boat dropped it when she came to borrow some coffee. It couldn't belong to Selena. I told you, she hasn't been here."

"Owen," Kira said softly, "We women notice certain things— jewelry for instance. I've seen this earring before. It's quite distinctive, with the red glass, isn't it?" She watched as he kept turning it in his hand. "I'm sorry, Owen, but I know Selena was wearing earrings just like this on Wednesday evening when I visited Angela. I saw them as she was leaving her house. She wore this one and its match—both of them."

Only the creaking of the boat and the lapping of the water against the hull broke the silence. She finally said, "Please, don't lie to me. Crazy as it sounds, if you're in trouble, I want to help." She didn't want to believe he could have done something as awful as the presence of Selena's earring suggested.

His face pale, Owen said, "I suppose I'll have to tell you the truth." He put the earring in his pant's pocket, as he got up and began wandering around the small cabin. Running his hands through his hair, he blurted, "God knows I didn't want this to come out."

His pacing eventually led him to the galley. Taking a position behind a counter and leaning on it for support he began, "All right. I did lie to you . . . to the police . . . to everyone. I felt pressured, with no other option." He shook his head as though to clear his thoughts. "When I heard what happened to Selena, I knew if I said she had been here Wednesday night the police would instantly suspect me."

"I don't fault you for being worried," Kira said softly. "Savarous would make anyone nervous. But you're still not explaining why she came here? I wasn't aware you knew her that well." By this time, Kira's hands, resting on the table, were becoming damp with perspiration and sticking to the glass top. She didn't want to know his secret, yet she had to find out what had happened. She'd hoped tonight might be the beginning of something special, but now . . .? The discovery of the earring was destroying her dreams for the future.

Owen sighed. "It's a long story." He opened a drawer, put something bulky in his pocket, then closed the drawer again. He began wiping the spotless countertop with a towel, before replacing the towel on its hook. Finally, he said, "You know Selena's husband was the skipper of one of my boats?"

"Yes."

"Well, after his unexplained disappearance, I felt partially responsible for his family's welfare. They were going to be hard-pressed for money until the insurance company was satisfied that he had died, not just disappeared. So . . . several times I gave Selena money. Not a lot, mind you, but I didn't want them to suffer."

Kira nodded. What he said sounded reasonable. Owen had the reputation of being a thoughtful person. That was one of his characteristics that had attracted her. His helping Selena went right along with what she had learned about him from Jackie and other people she'd talked with at the terminal. However, it still didn't explain Selena's presence here.

Owen continued, "I became concerned that Selena might be depending on my money a little too much. Then she showed up here Wednesday night." He paused and looked down at his hands that were slowly moving over the counter as though he still had the towel in them. "She wanted more money . . . a lot more." His eyes seemed to focus on the memory. "When I refused, she accused me of having something to do with Reynaldo and Jason's deaths."

He looked at her, as though to emphasize his surprise at what had happened. "For a moment, I was speechless. I couldn't imagine where she got that idea. That's when the argument began that was reported." He began prowling about the cabin again. "She threatened me with going to the police, telling them I was involved in her husband's death, and that I'd killed Reynaldo because he was going to finger me as a drug lord or something. I couldn't believe it! She thought I was involved with bringing drugs into Raven Creek and had dragged her husband in to help me. Good God, I wouldn't do that kind of thing." He abruptly stopped his pacing to face Kira. "I explained to her how I felt about drug trafficking, but I couldn't convince her. I suppose you don't believe me either?" His eyes appealed for understanding. "The police were already questioning me about Reynaldo's death. Selena's presence here would have been one coincidence too many. That Savarous is like a wolverine. He would have made my life hell."

The thought that Owen might be a killer started Kira's heart beating fiercely. She knew she was taking a chance by continuing this conversation, but felt she was on the verge of discovering something important to her future plans, and possibly to the police. She couldn't pull back. "But, Owen, now you are in a real mess. I want to believe you but . . ."

"But what?" Owen asked. He came over to the table, leaned down, and began to slowly gather the charts.

Shrinking a little from his nearness, she said, "The 'but what' is, why did you lie and keep Selena's visit here a secret? It might have meant more grief from Savarous, but anything is better than his catching you in a misstatement. And you still haven't explained how Selena came to lose the earring. Under normal activity, they don't just fall off."

"I have no idea why her earring came off," he said abruptly. His expression of mystified concern was almost convincing.

"None at all?" Kira tried to keep skepticism out of her voice. "I know Selena was in no mood for a friendly visit when she stormed out of her house that night. She said she wanted some answers. She may have gone to someone else first, but now I think her last stop was here."

Owen stared at Kira for a long moment, then said, "I'll admit we were both upset that night, but I had no reason to hurt her." He walked to the control station and placed the maps on the console. "Besides—she left the boat after our argument."

She unconsciously reached out a hand as though to detain him, then let her arm fall back to the table. "I think you did have a reason." She hated what she was going to say. "You've told me she talked of blackmailing you. Did she want drugs . . . or did she want a part of the action? Did she want a partnership, and threaten to go to the police if you wouldn't take her into the business?"

"Kira . . ."

She knew she must speak carefully. "A woman doesn't usually remove a single earring. She would be more likely to take off both of them and put them together either on a table or in her purse. I think this one may have been torn off . . . in a struggle." Her hands were shaking now. *How did I allow myself to get entangled in this conversation?* She went on, "The earring hook has been straightened, as though violently pulled from an ear."

"Kira, I wouldn't hurt Selena. You're way off the mark if you think any of this could be true."

She couldn't stop. "No, I think I've hit the target. I wouldn't be surprised if Savarous was coming to the same conclusion. He's a jerk, but he's a dogged jerk. And don't forget, Don saw you out driving the night Reynaldo was dumped on the conveyer belt. Remember? He mentioned it at lunch the other day. And then the story you told me about your truck possibly being used without your knowledge that same night. That was pretty thin."

Kira watched as sweat formed along Owen's hairline and begin to trickle down his cheeks. She suddenly realized she'd said far too much.

He gave her a look of icy appraisal. "Selena was different that night," Owen finally said. "I'd loaned her money and helped her manage after her tight-fisted husband died. Wednesday she suddenly became greedy and threatened me." Owen's eyes narrowed into slits as he continued his story. "In the end, she became too demanding. We argued and fought. My God, she was like a wildcat." He took a few agitated steps toward the galley, then abruptly turned back toward her. "Yes, I killed her. I didn't want to, but I had no choice." He was still for a moment, as though reliving those moments. "I couldn't let her leave here after her threats. Her death was regrettable, as was the killing of Reynaldo. He had been useful to me. He was reliable, the quiet type, not a person the police would suspect. And he had buyers all over town."

Kira couldn't believe what she was hearing. How could he be so cold-blooded, so devoid of feeling, so different from the man she thought she knew? Then she suddenly asked herself, *Why is he telling me all this? He must realize I can't keep something like this a secret?*

Owen continued in an impersonal tone, "Reynaldo said he wanted to become equal partners. I've since wondered if that was his idea or Selena's. It doesn't really matter. I was left with no choice but to act."

Kira knew that if she had any sense, she would run out on deck and scream for help. But she was frozen in place. "After tonight, and what you've said about Selena . . ."

Owen moved closer to her.

Kira saw a coldness in his expression she would never have imagined possible. She pressed her arms hard against the wicker chair, and said, a bleak quality in her voice, "I bet you had something to do with Jason's disappearance, too." She was afraid to move.

"Jason was not making enough to support his family, especially Selena. What a shame for him—but a blessing for my purposes." A muscle twitched at the side of Owen's mouth, as though he enjoyed that thought. "When he came to my office, I explained the financial facts of life to him. He saw he had no choice but to do what I wanted." As though to excuse himself, Owen emphasized, "I promised he would make enough money to pay his bills with ease."

"You had him backed into a corner."

"I sure did." His scowl deepened.

Kira wondered what a person should say when she has just heard the description of three murders?

"So, what are you going to do now that you've heard what's happened?" he asked in a low voice. "Go to the police? They won't believe you. You have no proof, no witness to what I've said."

Kira stared at him. "You've forgotten—I have Selena's earring."

"Your mistake. You did have it . . . now I do. I'm more sorry than I can say that you found it here tonight." In a flat tone, he added, "Unfortunately, the situation has irreversibly changed. I can't let you take your suspicions and knowledge away from here. I have too much at stake."

He suddenly moved to the back of her chair, grabbed her arm, and twisted it painfully up behind her. She struggled, but he was too strong, and he clearly knew the tricks of inflicting pain. With his other hand clamped in her hair, he dragged her from the chair, knocking it out from under her, and forced her across the cabin, down the steps, and into a stateroom. At first she was too surprised to scream. When she did take a deep breath to call for help, he jerked her arm up higher and ordered, "Shut up!"

Kira's shout was stillborn, turned into a whimper of pain.

In the stateroom, he threw her face down onto the bunk and removed a roll of duct tape from his pocket, the 'something' he had taken from the drawer in the galley. Kira heard the sound of ripping and struggled to twist off the bed, but he was too fast for her. He taped her hands behind her, then tightly bound her ankles. He finished by rolling her over and slapping a long piece of tape over her mouth. Both terrified and furious, she realized her growing affection for him had blinded her to the danger of trying to reason about murder.

He looked down at her, nodded as though acknowledging a job well done, then calmly turned and walked out.

Kira had heard that Alaska was held together with duct tape. Now, she believed it. Immobilized by the damn stuff, and feeling as hopeless and deep down scared as she could ever remember, she despaired of escaping, or even being able to signal for help, with this awful tape binding her and muffling her voice.

CHAPTER THIRTY-SEVEN

Kelly knocked on the side of the *Raven Witch*. He and Angela had come to see what was delaying Kira and Owen so long. Grinning to himself, he guessed that they were enjoying their time alone. He regretted the need to interrupt. However, Warren and Jackie were ready to return home and, having no clear idea of Kira's plans, had asked him to find out if they should wait for her.

When there was no response to his knocking, Kelly knocked again. Lights were on, so they must still be there. Then he spotted Owen in the cabin.

"Hey, Owen," Kelly called cheerfully. "We've been sent to ask if Kira plans to go home with Jackie and Warren, or will you bring her?" His hand on the railing, he prepared to climb aboard.

Owen quickly crossed the salon and slid open the door to the deck. In a perplexed voice he said, "Oh, hello, Kelly, Angela. I didn't expect anyone to come by." Responding to their questions, he said, "Kira isn't here. I don't know what to tell you. She left about ten minutes ago. Haven't you seen her?"

"We've been wandering about these floats ever since dinner." Kelly glanced at Angela, who nodded in agreement. "We haven't seen her. Are you sure she intended to come back up to the parking lot?"

"I don't know where else she would have gone," Owen said. At that moment Kelly heard a muffled thump from the far side of the hull. Owen stiffened, then relaxed again. "It's nothing. Just the fender on the other side of the boat," he said, not meeting Kelly's eyes.

His explanation didn't make sense to Kelly. It was low tide. The water was quiet. "May we come aboard?" Kelly asked. "Not finding Kira worries me." He leaned forward to step onto the boat. "I think we should talk this over. We may need to search for her."

"No need for that. I tell you, she isn't here."

Angela squeezed Kelly's hand, then said decisively, "We scouted all around on our way here and didn't see her. I'm worried."

Again, Owen said, his voice rising, "Kira isn't here."

Kelly's suspicions were aroused even more, as he saw a chair lying on its side and Kira's purse near it. "I don't think you're telling us a straight story," he said. "We want to look for ourselves . . . right now."

Owen shouted, "Like hell you are! Set foot on my deck, and I'll throw you into the bay."

Kelly turned to Angela. "Quick. Find help. Run!"

"No, you don't," Owen bellowed as he reached to grab Angela. He had a partial grasp on her arm, but was leaning too far over the edge of the boat and couldn't get a strong grip. He jumped onto the float to strengthen his hold, but she twisted away and ran.

Kelly leaped at Owen, knocking him off balance against the boat. Pushing away, Owen regained his balance and swung a right to Kelly's head. Momentarily staggered, Kelly went to his knees, but reached out to snatch at Owen's legs. Owen kicked at him, his shoe scraping painfully over Kelly's ear. Struggling to his feet, Kelly again flung himself at Owen, this time managing to push him toward the far end of the float.

They struggled up and down the length of the float—a mixture of flailing fists and wrestling moves. Owen was strong and heavier; Kelly, young and quicker on his feet. Owen grabbed Kelly's jacket and swung him around, trying to bash his skull against an anchor suspended at head-height from the pulpit on the bow of a boat. Kelly barely ducked in time to avoid being speared by one of the flukes. He swore, as he violently yanked his sleeve from Owen's grip. This abrupt movement again brought Kelly to his knees.

He struggled to his feet, but before he was able to reach Owen, the older man's foot slipped on a damp spot left over from all the rain. He lost his balance, tripped on the bull rail at the edge of the float, and fell back against a boat railing. Arms outstretched, he tried to regain his balance, but, continuing sideways, hit his head on the transom, rebounded from there to the swim deck, and finally tumbled into the dark water.

Kelly had fallen to his knees, exhausted. Suddenly concerned by the lack of sound or movement from the water, he stumbled to the edge of the float and looked over. In the shadow of the hull he saw Owen, face down, unmoving.

"Damn!" Kelly exclaimed. He jerked off his jacket and launched himself into the water. He didn't yet know what Owen had done to Kira, but wasn't about to let him drown before he got an explanation. He came up gasping for breath from the shock of the frigid water, and reached Owen in a few strokes, turning the inert form onto its back.

Frantically, he looked for signs of life and was relieved to see that, although unconscious, Owen still breathed. Slowly, keeping Owen's face out of the water, Kelly began maneuvering him back toward the edge of the float.

He heard his name shouted and looked up to see Warren and Jackie running toward him. Through chattering teeth, he called out, "Get help. This water is freezing. I don't know how long I can stay in here."

"I'll give you a hand." Warren knelt, reached down, and grabbed Owen's jacket collar. "Angela found us. We called 911. The ambulance should be here any minute. We probably shouldn't try to get him out. He might have a broken neck."

Kelly managed to gasp, "What's going on?"

"We left Angela up in the parking lot to direct the rescue squad. What in the world started all this?" Warren asked. "All Angela told us was that you were in trouble with Owen."

Still breathless from the cold and barely able to speak, Kelly said, "We argued, he tried to stop Angela from going for help. Then we fought. While I was down on my knees, he tripped or slipped, lost his balance and fell in. He hit his head as he was falling."

"Yes. We saw the fall as we were running down the ramp," Jackie said, approaching the two men. She was still breathing hard from her sprint.

"But where is Kira?" Warren asked, his voice harsh with concern. "Angela said you couldn't find her."

"We think Owen may have done something to her. He said she'd already left his boat—but I think she may still be there. Go look. I can hold out for a few more minutes."

"If he hurt Kira, I would just as soon let him sink," Warren said, his voice a low growl.

Jackie ran back along the float toward the *Raven Witch*.

CHAPTER THIRTY-EIGHT

Jackie scrambled aboard the *Witch* as fast as she could, almost tripping over the edge in her haste. She opened the main cabin door and called Kira's name. Silence. She looked around frantically. "What has he done to Kira?" she whispered. "Oh, please, God. Let me find her."

She called Kira's name again and this time heard thumping from below. Racing to the steps that led down to the staterooms, she saw a disheveled and bound Kira, attempting to inch her way up.

Jackie leapt down the stairs. "Oh, my God." With fumbling fingers, and saying, "Sorry. This is going to hurt," she tore the tape from Kira's mouth.

"Whew," Kira's voice quavered, when she was able to talk. "Am I glad to see you." Quickly stripping the tape from Kira's wrists and ankles, a badly-shaken Jackie demanded, "Are you all right? What happened? How did you end up like this?"

Through red and swollen lips, Kira replied, "I'm so relieved it's you that came. When I heard steps, I was afraid it was Owen. I was terrified he was returning to finish me off." She laughed brokenly, as Jackie helped her up to the salon. "I was determined to somehow make a noise or get up those steps. Something. Anything. I don't know what I would have done if the sliding doors were closed. I only knew I must get out into the light. When I heard Owen arguing with someone, then going out on the float, I hoped he was so diverted, he wouldn't think about locking the doors."

Rubbing Kira's wrists to restore circulation, Jackie said, "We've been so worried. You were gone too long. Come, sit here at the table a moment. Can I get you some water? Or there may be something stronger in the cabinets."

"Water is fine. That tape tore at my skin when you pulled it off." Kira touched her lips gently. "I thought I was going to smother. Now, tell me what's happened to Owen and Kelly? I thought I heard their voices on deck. That's when I kicked at the wall next to the bunk, trying to attract attention."

"Kelly and Angela came looking for you. You must have been taped up by then. Kelly didn't believe Owen when he insisted you weren't here, especially when he wouldn't let anyone onto his boat."

"Where's Owen now? He's dangerous."

"There was one hell of a fight. At the end, Owen tripped and fell into the water. He hit his head on the way down and was unconscious when I came to find you." Jackie gestured toward the salon door and gleefully reported, "He's not dangerous now. When you're feeling better, we can go see what's happening."

Moving toward the outer deck, Kira said, "I'm more than ready. Lord knows, I don't want to stay here any longer."

The sirens of official cars had reached a crescendo in the parking lot. The red lights of an ambulance flashed wildly. "Come on." Jackie put her arm around Kira. "I think the troops have arrived."

CHAPTER THIRTY-NINE

"I hear sirens." Warren said to Kelly. "Just hang on a little longer."

Kelly looked up to see Jackie and Kira hurrying toward them. Warren let go of Owen's collar and rose quickly from the edge of the float. "You found her," he exclaimed in relief, hugging Kira. "Where were you? Are you all right?"

Jackie explained, "When I found her, she was bound hand and foot with duct tape, inching her way out of a stateroom and trying to get up the stairs. She's shaken, but okay."

Jackie looked down at Kelly, still supporting Owen in the water. "As you can hear, help is almost upon us. How's he doing? Alive, I hope."

The EMTs hurried down the ramp and along the float to where the group waited. Before Kelly could answer Jackie's question, all of them were forced to draw back to make room for the ambulance team. Two men rolled a gurney loaded with rescue and resuscitation equipment. Another brought a backboard. Several other men accompanied them. Kelly shook violently from the cold and could only stutter answers to their questions. The EMTs slipped into the water to help position Owen's body on a backboard and strap him in place, so he could be lifted out of the water. Once Owen was up on the float, an EMT knelt beside him and checked his pulse. The inert form was lifted onto the gurney. He was breathing on his own, but they gave him oxygen and attached a cardiac monitor to check his vital signs.

His part in the rescue completed, Kelly fumbled his way up a rescue ladder attached to the side of the float. Warren picked up the jacket dropped when Kelly leaped in after Owen and helped him struggle into it. Angela, murmuring anxiously, buttoned it, as Kelly's fingers were too numb for the task. At that moment, Kelly was sure there were not enough coats in all Alaska to get him warm again. One of the rescue squad, seeing his distress, brought a blanket, which Kelly thankfully added over his jacket.

Jackie, who had been watching the activity on the float, chanced to glance toward the parking lot. "Oh, no. I don't believe it!" she exclaimed. Detective Savarous and Officer Winston were hurrying toward them. "Vultures at a feast," she said, under her breath. The officers first talked at length with the rescue team, then, apparently satisfied, approached the group around Kira to ask for details of the accident.

Still shivering, Kelly told of trying to find Kira, Owen's evasiveness and the ensuing struggle. Angela reported Owen's refusal to let them on his boat. Jackie explained about finding Kira. Warren detailed his calling for help, then rushing back in time to see Owen trip, knock against the transom and swim deck, before collapsing into the bay. He made it clear that Owen had not been pushed over the edge, but had lost his balance and fallen.

"I don't understand all this," Savarous said. "What was Owen Martin's reason for behaving in such a bizarre way? He would never do all you've accused him of. I can't believe it. He's a calm man, not given to this kind of rowdy behavior."

As the fire department team rolled Owen away toward the ambulance, it was Kira's turn to speak. "I think I can explain that. It all started when I sat on an earring . . .

CHAPTER FORTY

Friday

Five days later, many of the mural volunteers were gathered on the beach in front of Marty and Tom Engelmann's RV for a late day BBQ. The water lapped softly on the rocks of the shore. The sight of the late-arriving boats seeking rest in the harbor had everyone relaxed and in a carefree mood.

Talk centered on the painting of the mural and continued in a similar vein through most of the meal. It sharply changed direction when the pie was served. Angela expressed her relief that the conflict over her father's boat had faded away. It was as though her comment gave others permission to ask questions and speculate about the *Halibut*, murders and drugs.

Several of the people present knew little of the events of Sunday night, so Nathan's question, "What's the latest on the murder investigation?" loosened a barrage of questions about the unraveling of the Raven Creek nightmare.

"You probably read in the paper that the police solved the murder cases," Warren said. "But don't believe all you read. In truth, Kira did it for them."

At this, Kira recounted her visit to Owen's boat and finding the earring. She ended by saying, "I'm convinced that if Kelly and Angela had not come searching for me, Owen would have taken the boat out into the bay and tossed me over."

Jackie took up the story. "Fortunately, Angela and Kelly were suspicious. Kira owes her life to their acting on their doubts. The conflict ended with Owen unconscious in the water and Kelly keeping him afloat until the rescue squad arrived. When he regained consciousness, Owen said something that has now led to an investigation of Savarous. The little I've been told indicates that Savarous, himself, was involved with bringing drugs into Raven Creek. In fact, he may have been the one in charge, with Owen and Reynaldo working under him. Exactly which of them was the boss of the operation isn't clear yet." Jackie continued, "Savarous may have been involved with Jason's death last spring, and maybe Randy's, too, although his body hasn't turned up yet. The boy's fate may never be known."

At this Angela let out a cry. "You mean my father may really have been smuggling drugs, after all? How could he? He hated them, and what they do to people."

"Let's hope he wasn't involved," Kira said, "but if he were, you need to consider what might have driven him to do it. I think your father loved you very much, and wanted the best for both of you."

"I suppose you're right," Angela said reluctantly. "But it will take time for me to accept that he gave into such awful temptation. I just wish he hadn't felt he had to."

Kelly pulled her close.

"Seems like the mysteries of last week have been solved," Jackie said. "Owen is in jail, Savarous appears to be involved in the drug trade, and is about to follow him, and we all have produced an impressive memorial to the captains and crews who lost their lives in nearby waters."

Everyone raised glasses in agreement. Even Angela was able to smile.

After dark, they all gathered near the bonfire to ward off the coolness of the evening. Kira gazed at the surrounding mountains thrusting up from the darkening land, their tops reaching up to warm themselves in the last glow of the day. Silver splashes of reflected skylight from the ponds, randomly spread at their base, decorated the shadows. She looked around at the fading day and thought how fortunate the local people were to be surrounded by such beauty, even though it might occasionally be tarnished by greed and self-interest.

"This evening has been an experience I'll treasure from my visit here," Kira said. "In spite of this week's various tribulations, your beautiful, wildlife-filled land, and the wonderful people I've met since coming here, will remain a magnet for me when I go home to Arizona."

She realized she might never be able to come back in person, but knew she would often return to Raven Creek in memory.